Chip Hilton Sports Series

#14

W9-DIN-539

Tournament Crisis

Coach Clair Bee

Foreword by Jack McCallum

BROADMAN
& HOLMAN
PUBLISHERS

Nashville, Tennessee

0-8054-2093-2

Published by Broadman & Holman Publishers,
Nashville, Tennessee

Subject Heading: BASKETBALL—FICTION / YOUTH
Library of Congress Card Catalog Number: 99-051788

Library of Congress Cataloging-in-Publication Data
Bee, Clair.
    Tournament crisis / Clair Bee ; [updated by Randall and
Cynthia Bee Farley].
        p. cm. — (Chip Hilton sports series ; [14])
    Summary: Chip and his teammates come to the aid of
their Chinese American friend so that he can pursue an
education while also playing basketball at State University.
    ISBN 0-8054-2093-2
    [1. Basketball—Fiction. 2. Chinese Americans—Fiction.
3. Friendship—Fiction.] I. Farley, Cynthia Bee, 1952– .
II. Farley, Randall K., 1952– . III. Title.

PZ7.B38196Tp   2000
[Fic]—dc21   99-051788
                                        CIP

1 2 3 4 5 04 03 02 01 00

The Chip Hilton Sports Series

Touchdown Pass
Championship Ball
Strike Three!
Clutch Hitter!
A Pass and a Prayer
Hoop Crazy
Pitchers' Duel
Dugout Jinx
Freshman Quarterback
Backboard Fever
Fence Busters
Ten Seconds to Play!

Fourth Down Showdown
Tournament Crisis
Hardcourt Upset
Pay-Off Pitch
No-Hitter
Triple-Threat Trouble
Backcourt Ace
Buzzer Basket
Comeback Cagers
Home Run Feud
Hungry Hurler
Fiery Fullback

For more information on
Chip Hilton-related activities and to correspond
with other Chip Hilton fans, check the website at
www.chiphilton.com

TO
LEONARD MULHALL
AND HIS SON
TOMMY

CLAIR BEE
1957

TO
OUR DEDICATED HISTORY
AND ENGLISH PROFESSORS

at the University of North Carolina
at Charlotte—a great place to be students

CYNTHIA AND RANDY
JANUARY 2000

Contents

Foreword by Jack McCallum, *Sports Illustrated*

1. . . . . . **Time for Hoops!**
2. . . . . . **The Same Goes for Dribbling**
3. . . . . . **In the Tournament**
4. . . . . . **Coaching Is a Difficult Job**
5. . . . . . **Dribbling Wizard to Start**
6. . . . . . **Don't Knock the Rock!**
7. . . . . . **The Golden Rule**
8. . . . . . **Filial Piety**
9. . . . . . **"The Treatment"**
10. . . . . . **The Way It Was Meant to Be Played**

CONTENTS

11. . . . . . Subtle as a Technical Foul

12. . . . . . The Team's the Thing

13. . . . . . The Tea House

14. . . . . . We're in the Restaurant Business!

15. . . . . . 'Tis the Season for Giving

16. . . . . . There Was Something Magical

17. . . . . . Have a Friend, Be a Friend

18. . . . . . Beyond the Stars to Reality

19. . . . . . He Loves the Game

20. . . . . . Friendship Is Its Own Reward

21. . . . . . One More Shot

22. . . . . . We Learn from the Young

Afterword by Coach Marlo M. Termini

Your Score Card

About the Author

Foreword

IT'S SOMETIMES difficult to figure out why we became who we became. Was it an influential teacher who steered you toward biology? A beloved grandparent who turned you into a machinist? A motorcycle accident that forced you into accounting?

All I know is that in my case the Chip Hilton books had something—no, a lot—to do with my becoming a sports journalist. At the very least, the books got me to sit down and read when others of my generation were watching television or otherwise goofing off; at most, they taught me many of life's lessons, about sports and sportsmanship, about coaches and coaching, about winning and losing.

Also, the books helped me, quite literally, get the job I have now. Over two decades ago, when I was a sports writer at a small newspaper in Pennsylvania, I interviewed Clair Bee and wrote a piece about him and the Hilton books. For some strange reason, even before I met Clair, I knew I could make the story memorable, knew that meeting a legend like Clair and plumbing his mind for memories were going to be magic. They were. I sold the story to *Sports Illustrated,* and, partly because of it, I was later hired there full time.

To my surprise, and especially to the surprise of the editors at *SI,* the story produced a torrent of letters, hundreds of them, all written by closet Clair and Chip fans who, like me, had grown up on the books and never been able to forget them. Since the piece about Clair appeared in 1979, I've written hundreds of other articles, many of them cover stories about famous athletes like Michael Jordan, Magic Johnson, and Larry Bird; yet I'm still known, by and large, as the "guy who wrote the Chip Hilton story." I would safely say that still, two decades later, six months do not go by that I don't receive some kind of question about Clair and Chip.

One of the many fortunate things that happened to me as a result of that story was meeting Clair's daughter, Cindy Farley, and her husband, Randy, as well as others who could recite the starting lineups of Coach Rockwell's Valley Falls teams.

I am proud to have played a small part in the revival of Chip and the restoration of interest in Clair (not that real basketball people ever forget him). It's hard to put a finger on what exactly endures from the books, but it occurs to me that what Clair succeeded in doing was to create a universe of which we would all like to be a part.

As I leafed through one of the books recently, a memory came back to me from my days as a twelve-year-old Pop Warner football player in Mays Landing, New Jersey. A friend who shared my interest in the books had just thrown an opposing quarterback for a loss in a key game. As we walked back to the huddle, he put his arm on my shoulder pads and, conjuring up a Hilton gang character, whispered, "Another jarring tackle by Biggie Cohen." No matter how old you get, you never forget something like that. Thank you, Clair Bee.

JACK McCALLUM
Senior Writer, *Sports Illustrated*

CHAPTER 1

Time for Hoops!

CHIP HILTON looked at his mom just as the doorbell rang, searching her face for any of the signs of illness he had missed just one year ago. Shortly after Chip had returned to State University after that Thanksgiving weekend spent at home in Valley Falls, his mom had been diagnosed with cancer. And so had begun their greatest test since his father's death. An operation had cleansed her body of the invasion, and the outlook was positive. Now, a year later and with another Thanksgiving weekend drawing to a close, Chip breathed a prayer of gratitude.

"I love you, Mom," he murmured as he wrapped her in his arms for a farewell hug. "I'll call you as soon as we get back to the dorm. Take care of yourself and let me know what Dr. Nader says at your checkup."

"I will. But how about *you*? I wish you'd wait a week or two before reporting for basketball. The football season was long, and you've only had a few days' rest. Will you have enough energy for your classes and practice every afternoon and working in the evenings and then staying up late studying?"

Chip grinned. "Don't worry, Mom. I'll get plenty of rest—if sitting on the bench can be called rest. The basketball squad has been practicing since mid-October. That means the starting team is all set."

"Then you'll upset it," Mary Hilton declared confidently.

"I'll sure try," Chip said grimly. He gave his mom one last hug, patted a meowing Hoops on the head, and grabbed his backpack, which was filled with freshly washed and ironed clothes. "OK, hold it, Soapy, I'm coming!" Chip called as he raced down the hall to the front door.

Soapy Smith, dressed in a bright red and blue State sweatshirt, was anxious to get moving. "C'mon, Chip, everybody's ready to go. You're riding with me and Red in Speed's car. The sooner we hit the road, the sooner I can get the guys to stop for food!"

Chip shoved his backpack into the trunk of Speed's red fastback Mustang and turned to wave to his mom. The Valley Falls contingent, most of the group friends since elementary school, was packed into the two cars. Biggie Cohen, Joel "Fats" Ohlsen, and Tug Rankin were riding with Biggie's brother, Abe. Red Schwartz had claimed the Mustang's other front bucket seat as Speed Morris revved the engine. Chip and Soapy slid into the back. Then they all waved to Mary Hilton and disappeared around the corner just as the first snowflakes of the season began to blanket Beech Street.

Before they had driven even halfway to University, Soapy demanded a pit stop for food saying, "I'm wasting away to nothing, Speed!" At the service plaza, Soapy sprinted for the restroom, telling Speed to save him a seat in the restaurant. When he came out, Soapy was surprised to find Abe, Biggie, Chip, Tug, Red, and Joel standing huddled around a booth and blocking his view of the table.

As he sauntered up, the grinning group parted and Soapy barged through. He couldn't believe his eyes. Four of the most beautiful girls he had ever seen were crowded into the booth!

"Oh, yes!" Soapy voiced. Then he took it all in and spied Speed Morris. Speed was sitting at the end of the bench next to two of the girls, smiling smugly and assuring them he was extremely comfortable. "I have plenty of room," Speed said, winking at the dark-haired beauty on his right.

"Get up, you traitor! You were supposed to save *me* a seat!" Soapy yelled, grabbing Speed by the jacket. Soapy kept pulling until he won the round and had Speed out of the booth. Then he slipped quickly into the space next to the two girls.

He smiled ingratiatingly and introduced himself. "I'm Soapy Smith! And my *friend*," he said, indicating Chip and coolly ignoring the rest of his mesmerized friends, "is Chip Hilton, State's all-American quarterback. I guess you've heard of *him!*"

The smiles and nodding heads satisfied Soapy and brought a wave of color to Chip's face.

"Oh, I've read about *you*," the brunette next to the window said, smiling up at Chip. "You won the Thanksgiving day football game!"

"I saw you on TV," another said shyly.

"Yeah," Soapy added, "Chip beat A & M for the conference championship."

"Sure," Chip scoffed, his ears reddening with each

passing second, "I was the only State player on the field! I won the game all by myself!"

The girl directly opposite was studying Soapy's face intently. "I've seen *you* somewhere before," she said. Then recognition dawned. "I know," she continued quickly, "you make all those strange ice-cream concoctions at Grayson's, the soda fountain near campus!"

"Sweetest job in town," Soapy drawled. "Chip works there too. He's in charge of the stockroom."

Chip shifted his feet uneasily, trying desperately to think of an excuse to escape. Just then, Speed looked out the window and announced, "The snow's starting to stick. Let's order something to go and get on the road."

Chip breathed a deep sigh of relief and politely smiled at the girls. "Nice meeting you," he said. "Coming, Soapy?"

"Gimme a minute, Chip. Order me three slices of pizza to go and a large milk, will ya? Get something to snack on too. I'll pay you when we get to the car."

Chip made his way toward the line, passing Speed and a teenage boy selling candy for the local high school fund-raiser. They were deep in conversation. Chip was at the front of the line and about to order when Soapy came rushing up, followed by the same candy-selling teenager Speed had been talking to.

"Chip, you gotta save me," Soapy explained breathlessly. "Can you lend me ten dollars?"

"Sure. What for?"

"Well, it's those girls. The candy guy, this kid here, came along and practically forced me to buy a little box of candy for the girls—and you know how much he took me for?"

"Ten dollars."

"That's right. *Ten* dollars! And those gold diggers—"

"Those girls?" Chip asked with a smile.

"Yes! *Those* girls! They grabbed the box and opened it before I could do anything about it. And me with my wallet packed in the trunk of Speed's car."

Chip grinned. "Well, you asked for it, Soapy. Anyway, here's the money."

Soapy's sigh of relief came from his heart. "Thanks, Chip. You're a real friend. As far as Speed Morris is concerned, our friendship is a thing of the past. When I asked him to lend me the money, he seemed to think it was a big joke. All of them seemed to think it was funny. Some friends! Speed was still laughing when I left. And as soon as I got up to come over here, he moved right into *my* seat."

Soapy turned to the teenager. "Here's your money, and I hope the government puts your school's candy drive out of business for profiteering." Soapy turned around and glared out the window.

The boy grinned broadly and covertly slipped seven dollars into Chip's hand, motioning toward Soapy. Chip nodded in understanding.

On the way to the cars, Speed and the rest of the Valley Falls crowd chuckled and kidded Soapy as they ran and slid through the parking lot. Speed's snowball to Soapy's back added insult to his fury. The redhead immediately prepared to do battle, but Chip saved Speed from immediate snowball annihilation by playfully waving the seven dollars in the air. Soapy had been had! "Speed," Chip called, "I expected something like this from Red, not from you."

Soapy ruefully admitted the Valley Falls crew had played a good joke on him. The score for the day was tied: Speed 1, Soapy 1.

Back on the road, Chip ate his pizza and then contentedly settled down for a nap. Seconds later, it seemed,

Soapy was shaking him awake. "C'mon, Chipper, wake up! We're home!"

Chip pushed himself up and looked out the window as Speed pulled into his parking spot behind Jefferson Hall. "Not University already?"

"Yep, it's our own Almy Mammy!"

The Monday after Thanksgiving vacation, school was back in session and football was the big topic on campus—specifically, State's stunning upset over A & M on Thanksgiving day. The sensational victory had knocked the Aggies out of consideration for national honors and had earned the Statesmen the conference championship.

Student fans who couldn't make the trip to the A & M campus for the big game, televised nationally as the "Game of the Week," had watched it at home.

Chip had been a key figure in the great victory. He received so much attention in his classes and on the campus all morning that he decided to skip lunch and, to avoid more attention, study in the library until his chemistry lab that afternoon.

He found his favorite table unoccupied and concentrated on his work. When the librarian placed the new daily newspapers on the rack, Chip got a copy of the *Herald,* one of University's papers, and hid behind the big spread of the sports section. But even there he found no escape from football.

Football leaped out at him on both pages—in headlines, subheads, special columns, and pictures—and all proclaimed State's exciting Thanksgiving day victory.

"There must be *something* about basketball in the paper," he mused, turning to the back page of the section. There he found the sports news he was seeking.

TIME FOR HOOPS!

SOUTHWESTERN TO DEFEND TITLE
The Holiday Invitational Tournament

Nov. 29. Southwestern University announced today that the NCAA champions would defend their Holiday Invitational Tournament laurels in Springfield, December 28-31. Southwestern opens its conference season against Washington University and will go into the game carrying a record of thirty-seven consecutive victories.

Chip shook his head in admiration. "Whew! Some record," he breathed.

In the last column on the page he found a special story by Bill Bell, the *Herald*'s veteran sports editor.

TIME FOR HOOPS!
by Bill Bell

Basketball, overshadowed by State's dramatic football season, bounces back into the center of the State sports pageant this Wednesday when the Statesmen meet Southern University in Assembly Hall at 8:30 P.M. This will be the first contest of a tough twenty-six-game schedule. State's and Southern's freshman teams meet in the preliminary game at 7:00 P.M.

Coach Jim Corrigan has been drilling a squad of some twenty players and is concentrating on an all-veteran group of basketball specialists who are expected to take over where State's pigskin warriors left off, dominating the conference. The court cast includes three seniors: Kirk Barkley, Bradley Gowdy, and Andy Thornhill, and four juniors: Bill King, Dom Di Santis, J. C. Tucker, and Li Hong "Jimmy" Chung.

TOURNAMENT CRISIS

Barkley, Gowdy, Thornhill, and King were regulars last season. Jimmy Chung, back from two years in the military, is expected to fill the spot vacated by George "Ace" Grimes who graduated last June.

Chung has been sensational in the preseason drills and is certain of a trial with the starting five. The returning veteran is a master dribbler and possesses supreme confidence. Coach Jim Corrigan, without qualification, tabs Chung as one of the most outstanding players in the country.

Local sophomore Sky Bollinger is certain to make the squad. He's joined by other hopefuls: Brody Reardon, Rudy Slater, Nick Hunter, Rodney Early, Trey Kepley, Mike Gibbons, and Ted Kane.

Local gridiron fans will be interested to know that a trio of State football heroes will tug off their cleats and shoulder pads this afternoon, slip into basketball uniforms, and report to Coach Corrigan. The trio is headed by William "Chip" Hilton, the sensational sophomore quarterback who sparked the Statesmen to the conference championship and, in the process, earned all-American honors for himself.

Speed Morris, who scampered for the winning touchdown in the last second of play against A & M last Thursday, is a fast, aggressive hoopster and is set to make a strong bid for one of the varsity spots. Soapy Smith proved a sturdy, fighting hustler for Curly Ralston's rugged line this past fall, and these same talents may earn him a spot on the hoops squad.

Hilton played freshman basketball last season. The six-foot, four-inch star hooks with either hand, can bury the jumper, and can sink the threes as well. It is the consensus of many fans that the sophomore sensation is better in basketball than he is in football.

TIME FOR HOOPS!

If a newcomer is to break into a starting position on Jim Corrigan's all-veteran team, it most certainly will be Hilton. It wouldn't surprise me if Hilton took over top hoop billing honors as soon as he can substitute the feel of sneakers for cleats. Hardcourt fans will remember Hilton won the senior title in the AAU National Basketball Marksmanship Tournament.

There was more, but Chip had read enough. "On the spot again," he murmured. "A person doesn't make a basketball team just because he can shoot!"

CHAPTER 2

The Same Goes for Dribbling

MURPH KELLY, State University's head trainer, sighed wearily and closed the locker room door. Then he sat down on the edge of one of the benches. "There oughta be a law!" he growled. "Football season no more than ends and it's basketball. Then it's baseball and spring football and track and tennis and golf, *and* then it's the middle of summer and Ralston's calling out the football squad for fall practice! Hah! That's a laugh! Fall practice in the middle of the summer. I'll go crazy if I name all the women's sports going on too!" Easing himself back against the lockers lining the wall, he let his thoughts wander back over the long years and the growth in athletic programs during the time he had served as State's head trainer.

And that's the way Chip, Soapy, and Speed found him, deeply engrossed in nostalgic memories of State's glorious sports history. Chip and his friends paused by the door and waited for Kelly to acknowledge their presence.

"Well, what do *you* want?" he grumbled, swinging around to face the door. "Oh, it's you! Now what? You football guys were supposed to turn in your gear last Friday."

"We did, Murph," Chip said gently. "We're reporting for basketball."

"I know, I know," Kelly said testily. "I read that plug Bill Bell gave you today in the *Herald*. He a friend of yours?" He waved a hand to silence the reply and continued. "Don't you guys know when you've had enough?"

"Keeps us out of mischief, Murph," Soapy replied lightly.

"Nothing keeps you out of mischief, Smith. Well, I suppose I might as well get it over with. Take those three lockers over there by the door. How come you didn't get here on time? It's a poor way to start out."

"We all have our science labs on Mondays and Thursdays until four o'clock, Murph," Soapy explained. He paused and then continued dryly. "And this is Monday."

"I know, I know. Well, don't worry about it. I'm used to temperamental athletes. No real harm done anyway. Corrigan and Rockwell haven't shown up yet. Now, let's see . . . Hilton, size eleven shoe as I remember. . . ."

The three athletes dressed quickly, and Chip led the way to the gym. Their basketball shoes made no sound on the hardwood floor, and they reached the side of the court unobserved. Behind them, Murph Kelly followed quietly, and the group paused on the sideline to view the action on the court.

The squad had formed a semicircle under the far basket and was intently watching a slim, lithe player who was putting on a dribbling show. The performer's skill was amazing! The ball bounced this way and that, behind his back and between his legs, and from one hand to the other, all as if dribbler and ball were connected by a rubber band. The player was a stranger to Chip, but he warmed to the dribbler's broad grin as he tried to please his teammates.

Chip scanned the faces of the watching players. His face lit up as he recognized four of his teammates from the previous year's freshman squad. Sky Bollinger, Brody "Bitsy" Reardon, Rudy Slater, and Nick Hunter were standing shoulder to shoulder and slightly behind the varsity holdovers.

A shout of appreciation and a sudden burst of applause brought Chip's attention back to the dribbling performer. The dribbler was lying on his side on the floor now, but his uncanny control of the bouncing ball was as sure and precise as it had been while he was on his feet. "He's a great ball handler!" Chip murmured.

"Unbelievable," Soapy agreed. "Now I've seen everything!"

"That's Jimmy Chung," Kelly said. "He puts on a show every afternoon before practice. The players like it."

"Who wouldn't?" Speed whispered. "He's terrific!"

Just then, one of the other players sprang forward and tried to grab the ball. But he didn't have a chance. The dribbler twisted his body with the speed and grace of a gymnast. The ball magically appeared on the other side of his body, under the control of his other hand.

"Now you see it, now you don't!" Soapy added with a whistle of admiration.

The first player who had tried to intercept the ball was now joined by other members of the squad, and soon the entire group was chasing the agile entertainer. It was good fun, and the dark eyes of the dribbler sparkled with keen enjoyment.

"I read about him in the paper," Speed said, "but I thought it was a lot of nonsense. Where was *he* last year, Murph?"

"In the military. He played as a sophomore three years ago. He was just fair then, but he's picked up a lot of basketball since."

"Certainly knows how to dribble," Chip said. "He's another Marcus Haynes. Haynes has got to be older than the Rock, and he's still dynamic. I saw him on TV during the Basketball Hall of Fame inductions. The entire audience went wild when he dribbled all over the stage. I know I did!"

"I saw that too!" Soapy exclaimed. "The commentator talked about Haynes's days spent traveling all over the world with the Globetrotters. He's a real ambassador for basketball."

"What branch of the service was Chung in, Murph?" Speed asked.

"He was in the army. Some sort of a science specialist. He's smart! Too smart, sometimes. . . ."

The blast of a whistle brought their attention to the other basket where Jim Corrigan, State's varsity basketball coach, and Henry Rockwell, his assistant, were watching the exhibition. "All right, men!" Corrigan called. "Hit the bleachers!"

Murph Kelly led the way, and Chip and his two buddies sat down beside him in the third row of bleachers. Sky Bollinger and Bitsy Reardon moved up beside them, grinning warmly.

"Man, am I glad to see you!" Sky whispered. He nodded toward the veterans seated in the first row. "Those guys invented the game!"

"Sure love that ball," Bitsy observed softly. "They won't trust it with any strangers."

"And they sure think we're strangers," Sky added significantly.

"Your troubles are at an end, my friends," Soapy hissed. "We'll kill 'em!"

When the shuffling ceased, Coach Corrigan looped the whistle around his neck and cleared his throat. "Before we go to work, men, I want to introduce Chip Hilton, Soapy Smith, and Speed Morris. I guess most of you know them by reputation, if not personally. At any rate, shake hands with them and introduce yourselves."

Chip, Soapy, and Speed stood up awkwardly and shook hands with each member of the squad. Most of the players knew Chip, and their handclasps were firm and friendly. But when he reached the dribbler, Jimmy Chung merely nodded and deliberately avoided Chip's extended hand. Chip was puzzled and a bit nettled by the incident, but he put it out of his mind when Coach Corrigan blasted the whistle.

"All right, now, three lanes and make it good. I want to see some fast, snappy passes. Give them a lead and hit them high on the shot!"

The squad was in high spirits, driving hard for the basket, yelling for the pass, and cheering each shot. The ball flew fast and sure from player to player, the only disruption to the rhythm coming when Chip, Soapy, or Speed were directly in the action.

"Atta baby, Kirk! Nice shot!"

"C'mon, Andy! Hit me, baby! Hit me!"

"Nice goin', King. Gimme that ball!"

"I've got it, Brad! C'mon in, Jimmy! What a shot!"

"All right, J. C.! Nice rebounding!"

"Give it to Dom, Bill! Give it to him!"

THE SAME GOES FOR DRIBBLING

Bitsy Reardon was right behind Chip in the passing line. "See what I mean?" he murmured. "They don't even know we've got names."

Chip saw, all right, but he wasn't worried about names right then. He had found out in the first couple of minutes that he was far from being in shape. Football was tough, but this was tougher. In football, on offense, he could get a quick rest between downs, in the huddle, and coming up to the line. After Chip gained the starting quarterback role, Coach Ralston had used him for punts, field goals, and point-after tries. Then he could rest while the other team had the ball.

But in basketball, a player had to keep moving all the time and be on his toes every second! Offense *and* defense. This was hard stuff unless he had worked up to it through a long training period.

Corrigan was a good coach, and he didn't intend to run his new recruits into the ground and risk ruining their feet in the first few days. "Hold it!" he called. "Hilton, Smith, Morris! Drop out for a few minutes. Take a rest!

"OK! Nice going, men! Now let's have a fast ten minutes on the deep figure eight. Keep driving to the basket and then fan out to the corner and up the sides. Barkley, Thornhill, King, Gowdy, and Chung come to this end of the court.

"Rock, you take Di Santis, Tucker, Bollinger, Slater, and Reardon down to the other end. The drill is about ball movement. I want twenty passes before a shot. Let's go!"

Chip, Soapy, and Speed stood thankfully next to the bleachers beside the trainer. Murph was glumly watching the weave pattern the teams were executing.

"It's a veteran team, Chip," Speed said in resignation. "Looks as if the coach has his starting five all set."

"Hold it!" Chip warned. "Watch the drill! Corrigan will throw us off the squad before we're on it."

The five players Coach Corrigan was drilling were almost letter-perfect in the control-ball weave. They made few mistakes, and these were covered up so quickly they were hardly noticeable.

Kirk Barkley and Andy Thornhill were unquestionably fine players, and the three years they had teamed up in varsity play had given them a sixth sense, it seemed to Chip, where their moves were concerned. Barkley was the bigger of the two and, strangely enough, faster too. Chip judged he was about six-four, and he was clearly well proportioned. Thornhill looked about six-two and was sturdily built.

"Barkley's *good!*" Speed whispered.

"I like the way Bill King handles his weight in the pivot," Soapy said. "He must weigh 300 pounds!"

"About 250," Chip breathed. "He looks taller than Sky."

"Sky's six-nine," Speed said, "but King looks twice as big out there."

Chip divided his attention between Bradley Gowdy and Jimmy Chung. If he was to make a starting position on this team, one of those two would have to be benched.

"Gowdy's not so hot," Soapy muttered, as if reading Chip's thoughts. "Neither is Chung."

"Can't tell until you see them scrimmage," Speed said.

Down at the other end, Bollinger, Slater, and Reardon were having trouble. Even a novice would have noticed the difference in the passing of the two teams. Corrigan's squad handled the ball crisply and moved freely while Rockwell's group fumbled frequently because of erratic passing. J. C. Tucker and

Dom Di Santis were obviously upset and out of sorts because of the play of the three sophomores.

Corrigan kept them going, counting up to twenty-five, thirty, thirty-five, and finally up to sixty passes before the shot. Then he called time and both teams trooped wearily to the bleachers.

"I'm worn out just watching," Soapy said, breathing heavily in sympathy with the tired players as the three friends clambered onto the bleachers. "I'm beginning to think I'm an old man."

Corrigan walked in front of the bleachers. "Now," he said, twirling the ball in his hands, "while we're taking a breather, I want to talk a little bit about shooting. All this passing we've been practicing is of no value unless the shooter can hit. Now you men aren't bad shooters up to fifteen feet, but we haven't got a man on the squad who can hit consistently from the outside.

"Holding the ball and waiting for a good shot, while remembering the thirty-five seconds on the shot clock, is sound basketball, and you men do it well. But if we don't find someone who can hit from the outside or from the corners, we're going to have to face floating defenses and zones every time we step on the court.

"Now perhaps this isn't fair, since this is Hilton's first day at practice, but he's got the form and the best shot I've ever seen. So I'm going to ask him to demonstrate. All right, Chip?"

"Soapy's a better shot, Coach."

Corrigan smiled. "I've never seen Smith shoot, Hilton, but I *have* seen you."

"Go ahead, Hilton!" Kelly growled. "Show 'em how to shoot!"

Chip stepped carefully down through the players and took the ball. His heart was thumping like the big bass drum at a football game, and while he waited for Corrigan to continue, he twirled and tested the ball in his long fingers.

"Don't worry about making the shot," Corrigan directed. "I'm interested only in form and mechanics. Backcourt men, take a good look at the mechanics of the shot. One of the managers will pass the ball back after Chip shoots."

Andre Gilbert dropped back under the basket and waited expectantly while Chip bounced the ball on the floor three or four times. Chip got set and let the ball go from about fifteen feet. He missed the whole works, basket and all. He fired two more with the same result.

"Try it in slow motion, Chip," Corrigan said kindly, "and loosen up." He turned to the bleachers. "Now let's check the shot. Chip's feet are about eight inches apart and nearly on a line. His knees are flexed, and his body is inclined forward. The elbows are close to his sides, and the ball is held with the fingers spread well—and even with his eyes.

"Note Chip's concentration on the basket. He's aiming the ball just as you would aim a gun; he's focusing his eyes on an imaginary spot in the middle of the ring."

Chip had been self-conscious in the beginning, but as Corrigan talked, his tension vanished.

"Now then," Corrigan continued, "watch how Chip releases the ball. He takes a little hop from the floor and his hands follow through after the ball, as if he is trying to reach up and grab the rim of the basket or put his shooting hand inside the basket."

This time the shot was too long. The rebound carried the ball straight back to the spot from which Chip had released the ball. Jimmy Chung convulsed and covered his mouth with his hand, but his laugh was clearly audible.

THE SAME GOES FOR DRIBBLING

Corrigan gave Chung a long, hard look and turned back to Chip. "Go ahead," he said encouragingly, "hit a few. You can do it."

Chip was loose and in dead earnest now, and his form began to tell. He made the first shot, took a long stride back until he was a good twenty-five feet from the basket, and hit another. Then he began to move around the three-point arc, dropping the ball cleanly through the hoop with each pass from Andre. All that could be heard now was the swish of the net as the shots zipped through the cords.

"Laugh that off!" Soapy hissed, glaring at Jimmy Chung.

Shot after shot ripped through the net. Then someone began to applaud. By the time Chip reached the corner, every player in the bleachers—except Jimmy Chung—was giving him a big hand.

Corrigan was smiling proudly, and when Chip sank the last shot from deep in the corner, he called, "Nice going, Chip. I knew you could do it."

Chip hurried back to the bleachers, self-conscious once again but happy that he had been able to come through. As he passed Jimmy Chung, he could not restrain a glance at the little dribbler. Jimmy's dark eyes narrowed, and it was obvious he was angry.

"There's more to basketball than practice shooting, Hilton," Chung sneered.

"You're right, Jimmy," Chip agreed amiably. "I guess the same goes for dribbling."

CHAPTER 3

In the Tournament

LI HONG "JIMMY" CHUNG'S head jerked around, and he eyed Chip's progress up the bleachers. Anger clouded his face, and his lips trembled with fury. Then Corrigan called the two teams back to the floor for a scrimmage. Jimmy Chung turned away.

"Don't worry about him," Kelly murmured as Chip sat down. He tapped his head significantly. "Oversized," he whispered.

"Did you hear him?" Soapy growled angrily, elbowing Speed. "What's that all about? What's up with that guy?"

"Murph has him pegged," Speed said. "He's too smart. Chip will take care of him."

Out on the court, Sky Bollinger lined up against Bill King, and Chip had a chance to compare the two centers. Sky was just as tall, but King's bulk made the sophomore look almost frail. Di Santis paired up against Barkley, and the two appeared evenly matched. Rudy Slater, at six-ten, towered over Andy Thornhill, who was an even six feet. J. C. Tucker was slightly shorter than Bradley Gowdy, but Jimmy Chung seemed at least a head taller than Bitsy Reardon.

"I hope Bitsy shows him up," Speed said.

But the reserves were no match for the experienced varsity returnees. Barkley, Thornhill, and Gowdy had played together for three years and knew their screens and plays perfectly. They held the ball until they got a sure shot close to the basket.

"Terrible basketball to watch," Murph Kelly whispered. "Almost as bad as A & M!"

"Don't they ever use a fast break?" Chip asked.

Kelly shook his head. "Nope, never!"

Jimmy Chung lost no time in trying to show up Bitsy Reardon. He took advantage of every opportunity to maneuver Bitsy into Bill King. King kept on the move, sliding from side to side across the free-throw lane and setting up picks and blocking posts for his teammates, but Jimmy did all the driving. He kept on top of the ball by reversing when he was going away from a pass and maneuvering himself into position for a shot whenever he got a half-step advantage on Bitsy. Most of his shots were forced, but he was outjumping Bitsy and getting the shots away. And some were hitting.

"Point crazy," Speed asserted.

"Corrigan won't let him get away with that very long," Kelly said. "He's trying him out."

Late in the scrimmage, Corrigan excused Di Santis, Tucker, and Reardon and replaced them with the three newcomers. Now the reserve team on the floor was made up of the same personnel who made up the freshman team the previous year, with the exception of Reardon.

There was a bit of confusion about the matchups. Chip walked over to Bradley Gowdy, who was about the same size, but Jimmy Chung trailed Chip purposefully and belligerently, motioning to Bradley to take the other guard position. "I want to play against the greatest shooter in the world," he said sarcastically, winking at Gowdy. "C'mon, Hilton. Teach me how to shoot!"

"Some other time," Chip replied calmly.

Speed matched up against Gowdy, and Soapy moved over beside Barkley. Then Corrigan tossed up the ball. Surprisingly, Sky Bollinger outjumped King and got the tap. Rudy Slater came in high and hard, took the ball, and immediately flipped it to Chip. It seemed like old times to Chip as he winged the ball to Soapy in the corner and set up a screen for Speed behind Gowdy.

Speed reacted like a flash and drove so hard for the basket that Jimmy Chung didn't have time to switch. Soapy shot a fast lead pass to Speed, and the flashy speedster scored.

"My, that was easy!" Soapy exulted. "Shall we try it again?"

The exuberant Soapy should have kept quiet. Corrigan blasted his whistle angrily and made the reserves walk through the entire maneuver in slow motion. Then he turned to Chung.

"That was your play, Jimmy. The back man always calls the switch, and you should have been watching for the pick. The next time your opponent sets up a post block behind one of your teammates and you think the cutter will get away, call the switch and call it loud! Then pick up the cutter and stick with him. Understand?"

That incident fired up the varsity players. They poured it on the hapless sophomores, holding the ball on the offense until they cleared a man for a wide-open shot. On the defense, they used a loose man-to-man alignment that was almost a zone.

Chip was almost six inches taller than Jimmy and could easily have gotten his hook shot or jumper away, but he decided to play a team game and sharpen his passing. So he continued to feed his teammates and set up the picks and blocks.

Chung was quick to realize what Chip was doing and began to play a tight defense, taunting Chip in a low, sarcastic voice. "Why don't you shoot, Hilton? Or can't you hit under pressure?"

Chip didn't like the gibes. He wanted to accept the challenge, but he kept his cool and continued to concentrate on passing and screening. A few seconds later, when Chung played sleeper and caught him napping, Chip really grew hot. Chung floated away from Chip and turned his head. Chip relaxed and passed the ball cross-court to Speed.

As soon as Chip released the ball, he realized his mistake. Jimmy yelped gleefully, dove for the ball, and got it! He continued to chortle sarcastically as he dribbled furiously toward the varsity basket.

Chip recovered quickly and took off after the speedy dribbler at full speed. Running smoothly, he gradually closed the gap. A step inside the free-throw line, Chung took off for what appeared to be a simple layup and an easy two points. Then Chip cut loose, turned on the gas, and timed his leap perfectly. His hand was even with the basket when the ball left Jimmy's fingertips, and the interception was easy.

Jimmy Chung's teammates had followed the wild drive up the court, and when Chip turned, he saw Speed all alone under his own basket. The rest was automatic. Chip fired the ball the length of the court and Speed dropped it in the basket.

The blast of Corrigan's whistle was far too loud to mean anything except displeasure. "All right!" he shouted. "Time!" He walked up the court until he was next to Jimmy Chung. "Now just what kind of basketball are we playing out here, Chung? *Your* kind or *my* kind? How many times have I told you we're not using the fast break? Tell me, how many times?"

"I'm sorry, Coach. I forgot. I—"

"That's right! You forgot *that* and the rest of your teammates too! Just because you were hot with Hilton and wanted to make a fancy play!"

Corrigan pivoted abruptly away from the chagrined dribbler and cut loose on Bradley. "And you, Gowdy! You've been playing possession basketball for three straight years, right?"

A subdued Gowdy nodded. "Yes, Coach."

"Then why didn't *you* stop Chung? And if you couldn't do that, why didn't you cover the backcourt? As a back-court player, you're responsible for defensive balance, right?"

"Right! My mistake, Coach."

Not a player moved as Corrigan glanced from one varsity player to another. He was visibly angry. After a long, heavy silence he continued. "Basketball is played with the head as well as the arms and hands and legs and feet. Smart players make good players, and players who can't restrain their impulses make poor players. All right, that's all! Think it over and come back here tomorrow afternoon prepared to play the kind of basketball we've been practicing for the past five weeks! Good night!"

Chip and Soapy dressed hurriedly and set out for Grayson's at Tenth and State. On the way they reviewed the practice, discussing the style of play. "Back to the old grind," Soapy said wearily. "We've been gone four days, but it seems like yesterday. You think we'll ever get through college, Chip?"

Chip nodded. "Absolutely! And before you know it, we'll be wondering where all those great college days went. Wonder how Fireball and Whitty have been doing with us gone?"

"They probably own the place by now," Soapy replied grinning.

The two lifelong friends and college roommates for one and a half years matched strides without speaking for a time, each deep in his own thoughts. Soapy broke the silence. "Why didn't you show him up?"

"Who?" Chip asked innocently.

"Duh-h-h! You know who! You gonna let him get away with the stuff he pulled tonight?"

"I don't think it's too important, Soapy. There's room for everybody on the squad."

Soapy shook his head. "Uh-uh! That's where you're wrong. There's only room for twelve. And twelve from eighteen leaves six. And six somebodies have gotta go."

"I know, Soapy. We've got to fight, that's all."

"You mean *I've* got to fight!"

Chip slapped Soapy on the back. "That, my friend," he said fondly, "is one of the things you do best!"

A few minutes later they were at Grayson's. As soon as they passed through the door, Fireball Finley spotted them. "Well, look who's here!" Finley yelled. "Hey, Whitty! Look! The reinforcements from Valley Falls have arrived!"

Chip and Soapy were greeted by employees and customers alike. Mitzi Savrill, the petite cashier and love of Soapy's life, hugged them and assured them that Grayson's had been deserted and was practically bankrupt. "The boss was thinking about telling you to take another month," she said, waving a hand toward the college students who jammed the store, filling every table and booth and gathering three-deep around the old-fashioned soda fountain as well. "Look! The place is practically empty."

Chip and Soapy took the hint!

Soapy sprinted to the employee lounge to change into his uniform, and Chip headed to the stockroom. In addition to its pharmacy side, Grayson's offered some of the best food in town, and it was the most popular meeting spot for the college crowd in all of University. In addition to the great food, George Grayson had installed a big-screen TV that was always tuned to the latest game or sporting event.

Chip found his helper, fifteen-year-old Isaiah Redding, in the stockroom. Isaiah's serious face brightened like a hot July sun breaking through the clouds. "Chip! Am I glad to see you! I'm swamped! I never missed anyone so much in my life!"

Owner George Grayson opened the door quietly and stood listening. "That goes for all of us," he added. "Isaiah's been doing a fine job, Chip, but all this is a little over his head, especially the computer data entry for the inventory."

Chip whirled around. "Mr. Grayson! I'm sorry. I'll make up for it."

Grayson smiled. "Don't worry about it. Have a nice Thanksgiving?"

"Yes, sir! I guess I was a little selfish—"

"Nonsense. How's your mother?"

"She's fine. She said to say hello to you and Mrs. Grayson."

"I read in the paper you were out for basketball. How did you make out?"

"Fine, Mr. Grayson. Soapy and I both made out pretty good. Coach went easy on us today since it was our first day of practice." Chip fumbled for the words to express his feelings. "That is, we reported for practice. But Soapy and I were talking, and we thought perhaps it wasn't fair to you—being away from the job so much. Basketball isn't nearly as important to us as our jobs. Honest!"

Grayson smiled and shook his head. "That's where you're wrong, Chip. Basketball is important. Right now the most important thing for all of us—you, Soapy, and me—is for you two to make that basketball team. I mean it, Chip. So you just forget all about being away from the job and make the team! OK?"

Chip couldn't find words to reply, so he made up for it by working the rest of the evening as if his life depended on catching up. He entered the accumulated invoices and inventory on the computer and properly stored the supplies that had arrived during his absence.

He was so engrossed in his work that 10:30 snuck up on him, and he was shocked when Soapy, Fireball, and Philip "Whitty" Whittemore showed up already out of their Grayson's red and blue polo shirts and white slacks and back in jeans, sweatshirts, and jackets. The four coworkers and friends headed wearily for Pete's Place, their usual afterwork snack site.

Pete greeted them warmly. "Hey! Look who's here! Chip! Soapy! About time you guys showed up! The place hasn't been the same. Soapy, they wanted me to cut back on the food inventory until you returned. Right, Fireball, Whitty?"

Chip had no difficulty falling asleep that night. When he awakened Tuesday morning, Soapy was already up, his bed empty. Chip got up slowly, painfully aware that his muscles were tight and stiff. Before he finished dressing, Soapy was back.

"Hey, Chip! You see the paper?"

"What are you talking about? How could I see the paper?"

"Well, take a look!"

"No, you tell me. What is it?"

"State's in the tournament!"

"What tournament?"

"You know the Holiday Invitational? The tournament they hold in Springfield during the Christmas holidays? Well—" Soapy paused dramatically and then continued with a rush—"State's been invited! Honest! State's been invited to participate and the invitation's been accepted! How about that?"

Chip's indifference vanished. "You're kidding!"

"No, I'm not! Honest! It starts on Monday, December twenty-seventh and goes through the thirty-first. The defending champions are Southwestern. They've won it four straight times! And they've got the same team back that won it last year."

"I guess they're pretty good."

"Pretty good? Chip! Listen! They've won 37 straight games and 130-something in a row at home. And listen to this! They've won the NCAA three times this decade and the Holiday Invitational four *straight* times!"

"What other teams are in the tournament?"

"College of the West, A & M, and Southeastern," Soapy turned back to the paper. "And listen to this! 'Southwestern's championship five is made up of five seniors who have put together the greatest basketball record in college history. Every writer in the country picks them to repeat in the Holiday Invitational Tournament and the NCAA championships.'"

"Upsets happen, Soapy," Chip stated quietly. "Winning any tournament is a tough assignment, and the Holiday Invitational will have the pick of the country lined up."

"I know, but a team like Southwestern *has* to have what it takes."

Chip nodded and changed the subject. "We've got a tough assignment too. I didn't tell you, but last night Mr. Grayson said the most important thing we have to do right now is make the varsity."

"You think he was kidding?"

"I know he wasn't. He was dead serious."

CHAPTER 4

Coaching Is a Difficult Job

SOAPY SMITH was a good basketball player. But he wasn't outstanding. And unlike most players with average skill, Soapy knew his limitations. But he loved basketball, and when he played, he gave it every ounce of his enthusiasm, spirit, aggressiveness, and ability. In fact, Soapy was usually enthusiastic about everything; he kept his spirits high and met adversity or good fortune with a smile. But not this morning.

At breakfast, while Chip was reading the paper, Soapy was methodically counting on his fingers, over and over again. His brow was creased, and he was obviously mulling over something extremely important.

"Now what? Is this some psychology assignment?" Chip asked and then caught the seriousness in Soapy's eyes. "What's up?"

"You know," Soapy said accusingly. "Basketball! Basketball and Grayson's and Mr. Grayson and a college education."

"I don't get it."

"Well," Soapy explained patiently, "you said that Mr. Grayson said the most important thing we had to do was make the basketball team, right? So, figuring my chances to do that, I'm wasting my time. I'd better pack up."

"I still don't get it. What are you talking about, Soapy?"

"Listen!" Soapy rested the elbow of his left arm on the table and counted off a finger as he named each player. "One, Kirk Barkley. A veteran and good, right?"

Chip nodded. "Right."

"Two, Andy Thornhill. And he's a senior and good. The same goes for Gowdy, King, Di Santis, and Tucker. That makes six veterans and doesn't include Chung. Corrigan's already tabbed him as one of the best and that's seven."

Chip started to say something, but Soapy shook his head and continued. "Take the sophomores. You're a cinch! And so is Sky Bollinger and Rudy Slater and Speed and Bitsy Reardon. And that's twelve any way you figure it.

"That leaves me with good ole unlucky number thirteen, and that's out, so I'm out! Even if I was good enough to beat out Early, Kepley, Kane, and Gibbons." He shook his head mournfully. "It ain't good."

"Maybe the coach will carry more than twelve players, Soapy," Chip offered.

"Not a chance. I asked Murph Kelly, and he said Corrigan doesn't like big squads. Nope, I'm dead. Valley Falls, here I come!"

"What do you mean, 'Valley Falls, here I come'? It's not quite that bad. Mr. Grayson didn't mean 'make the team, or else!' He was just trying to tell you and me not to worry about our jobs. That's all."

TOURNAMENT CRISIS

Soapy pressed his lips into a thin line. "I'm not so sure. I can't make that squad, Chip. I know it."

"We'll see," Chip said quietly. "I think you underestimate yourself. Now forget about basketball and finish your breakfast."

Chip resumed reading, turning the pages of the *News* until he came to the sports page. And there, almost as if Soapy had written the article, was confirmation of the redhead's fears.

STATE READY FOR BASKETBALL OPENER
Meets Southern Tomorrow Night at Assembly Hall
by Jim Locke

State University will field a veteran team tomorrow night against Southern in Assembly Hall. Coach Jim Corrigan has been working three seniors and two juniors as a unit for the past several weeks and has indicated that he will start the same five who carried the load most of last year.

The only newcomer is Li Hong "Jimmy" Chung, and he can't really be considered a newcomer since he was a member of the squad three years ago. The combination starting tomorrow night has Kirk Barkley and Andy Thornhill at forwards, all-conference Bill King at center, and Bradley Gowdy and Jimmy Chung at guards.

Other veterans who will most certainly see action, according to Corrigan, are J. C. Tucker and Dom Di Santis. The squad will probably be rounded out with five sophomores from last year's freshman team: Sky Bollinger, local high school phenomenon; Rudy Slater, outstanding rebounder; Bitsy Reardon, last year's captain and second leading scorer; and two of State's brightest young football stars, Chip Hilton and Speed Morris. . . .

Chip glanced at Soapy, hastily folded the paper, and slipped it behind him on the chair. "Come on," he urged, "we're going to be late for class."

They found the campus buzzing. The big topic was basketball. King Football is dead! Long live King Basketball!

"Southwestern will walk right through that tournament."

"How about A & M? And College of the West? And Southeastern and Deacon and Wilson State? They're not pushovers!"

"They're not Southwestern either."

"What's the matter with State? We've got everybody back."

"Won't get past the first round. Just an excuse for a trip. They have to have *someone* to fill out the draw."

"Well, we'll know tomorrow night."

"We'll know more next Wednesday when we play Southwestern."

"Be a slaughter! No one, but *no* one, beats Southwestern on their home court. They've won a couple hundred in a row at home."

"Not quite, but they've won a lot."

Chip, Soapy, and Speed reported for basketball an hour early that afternoon. Their muscles were tight, so Murph Kelly gave them a ball and told them to run their stiffness out. Once in the gym, they stretched out, took ten laps around the floor, and then began practicing their shots.

A little later the other players began to show up, one by one. Jimmy Chung came out on the court dribbling wildly. When he saw Chip, he dribbled over beside him. "I'm ready, Hilton," he said. "Show me how to shoot! You said yesterday you would teach me some other time. *This* is some other time."

Chip smiled amiably. "I don't think I could teach you anything about basketball, Jimmy," he said. "You've had a lot more experience than I have."

Every player on the court was conscious of the conversation and its implications, but each continued shooting and talking as if nothing unusual was taking place. That is, everyone but Soapy Smith and Speed Morris. They watched every move Jimmy Chung made.

"How about baby jumpers?" Chung suggested, dribbling in from the corner, setting, and dropping the ball cleanly through the basket. "All right?" he gibed, recovering the ball. "Or am I using the wrong *form?*"

"Looks pretty good to me," Chip said.

"Well, how about a jumper?" Chung dribbled back to the center of the court and then drove for the free-throw circle at full speed. He stopped suddenly, leaped into the air holding the ball a full arm's length above his head, and released it at the top of his jump with a flick of his fingers. The ball went spinning away, true and straight and right through the hoop.

Jimmy landed on the court and turned, grinning in fake humility. "All right?"

"Perfect," Chip said calmly, conscious that Chung was trying to bait him. But Chip was also aware that controlling his emotions would have a greater effect on the dribbler than a burst of angry words.

Corrigan appeared at that instant and sent the players into his three-lane warm-up drill. Chip breathed a sigh of relief.

Practice was almost a repetition of the previous day's

workout. Corrigan used Chip, Soapy, and Speed sparingly, but he had no mercy for the rest of the squad. He drilled the team at full speed for an hour and a half. Then he sent everyone to the bleachers.

Chip had a presentiment and fervently wished he could stop what was coming. His fears were quickly realized.

"Men, coaching is a difficult job. There is little gratification, even in winning games, because there is always the next one, which may be the killer. Losing is bad. But cutting a squad is worse.

"I've spent—Coach Rockwell and the other coaches and I have spent—many long hours trying to decide who should be kept on the squad. This is, as you know, the third and final cut. The other two cuts were bad enough, but this is the worst of all, chiefly because there is such a narrow margin of superiority between many of those who will remain on the team and those who will be asked to leave."

Chip was staring straight ahead, trying to breathe naturally. On either side, he could hear the tense, measured breathing of Soapy and Speed, and he knew they were having the same difficulty.

Corrigan's voice hardened. "We thank you all for coming out for the team, and we wish we could keep you all. Hunter, Early, Kepley, Gibbons, Kane, and Smith, we hope you will try again next year."

It was done! Chip let out a deep breath and reached over and gripped Soapy's knee. Speed lowered his head glumly and snapped a tight fist into his open hand.

Corrigan wasn't through. He began to speak again, and Chip wanted to yell out that he had said enough, should let it stand and forget the details.

But the words bit through. "With respect to you, Smith, Coach Rockwell and I both feel you haven't had a fair chance. We hope you will understand that it was necessary for us to make the decision before our first game. I'm truly sorry you couldn't be with us during all of the preseason practices. . . .

"However, if it's any consolation, Coach Rockwell would like you to report to him on Thursday when the freshman team meets for practice. He has some scouting in mind for you, Smith."

Corrigan took a deep breath and continued. "All right, you men are excused."

Chip tightened his grip on Soapy's knee. "Wait for me, will you, Soapy?"

Soapy nodded and swallowed. "Sure, Chipper," he managed, rising stiffly to his feet. "I'll wait."

Chip was thinking of the story he had read that morning in the *News.* "Jim Locke knew," he whispered to himself. "Corrigan gave him that list yesterday. Now I wish I *had* let Soapy see it."

Chip and Speed didn't get much of a workout that afternoon. Both were relieved; there wouldn't have been much fun in it. Late in the practice, Chip and Speed replaced J. C. Tucker and Bitsy Reardon, and Jimmy Chung again leeched onto Chip. But this time, Corrigan was watching every move he made, and Chung played it straight. Jimmy concentrated on his game and never said a word.

Chip could sense Jimmy's animosity and see the dislike in his eyes and grimly set jaw. He was glad when Corrigan called it a day.

Chip and Speed showered and dressed quickly and found Soapy waiting. The three buddies walked slowly across the campus and down Main Street to Grayson's. Soapy did all the talking, but it was painfully obvious that his overly cheerful voice and lighthearted attitude were an affectation, a front for his injured spirit. Speed left them at Main and Tenth, and Chip and Soapy went to work. It was a long evening.

That night after work, Chip, Soapy, Fireball, and Whitty headed for Pete's Place, each trying to cheer Soapy up without making it apparent. But they were poor actors, and it was Soapy himself who saved them from the awkward situation. He stopped them outside the restaurant.

"*Look,*" said Soapy, "let's cut out all the tiptoeing around it. I wasn't good enough, and I got cut, and that's that! Now if you guys will forget the whole thing, *I'll* feel a lot better.

"Anyway, I'm not quitting. I'll help Coach Rockwell out with whatever he wants me to do, and I'll be on that varsity yet! If not this year, then next year. And if not next year, the year after. Mark my words, there will come a day when Jim Corrigan and Henry Rockwell will both thank their lucky stars that good ole Soapy Smith was around to save the day."

That did it!

"Oh, sure!" Fireball whispered breathlessly. "The score will be tied. There will be less than a second to play, and Corrigan will run out on the court and yell time! And then he'll have Soapy Smith paged over the sound system.

"Then *you*—" he paused dramatically and tapped Soapy on the chest, "*you* will leap from the audience and—"

"Hold it!" Whittemore said quickly. "Then the school band will play the theme from *Rocky!*"

Fireball apologized profusely. "Excuse me. You're correct, Whitty. Slight omission. I'm not myself tonight . . . and then Soapy will hold up both hands for silence. And when the only sound heard is the rippling of the basket cords in the wind, Soapy will turn his back to the basket—"

"I know!" Whitty interrupted. "He'll turn his back and bounce the ball through his legs and through the basket and win the game and—"

"And they'll hang his shoes in the library!"

"The zoo!"

"The library!"

"The zoo!"

Soapy made a dash for the door to Pete's restaurant, turned, and thrust his arms in the air in his best Rocky pose. "Oh, baby!" he shouted. "I'm a hero! I'm a hero!"

Inside, Nick Hunter and several of his friends were hunched together in one of the booths. Nick greeted Soapy like a long-lost friend, although the two had never been close. "Hey, Soapy. What did you think of Corrigan's surgery this afternoon?"

Soapy shrugged. "You mean being cut from the squad? So what! Part of the game."

"Personally, I'm kind of glad," Hunter said. "I didn't feel too good about playing on the same team with a foreigner anyway—"

Before Soapy could reply, Chip interrupted, stepping between his friend and Hunter. "Jimmy Chung isn't a foreigner," he said quietly. "He was born here, and he served a full tour in the army. His father and mother were naturalized in this country."

"Big deal! What does that make him?"

"It makes him an American citizen. He's just as much an American as you or me."

CHAPTER 5

Dribbling Wizard to Start

PETE THORPE was proud of his restaurant. The equipment was well worn and the decor plain, but Pete kept everything scrupulously clean, and the atmosphere was comfortable. Although he drew a small number of the college students, Pete relied primarily on University residents for customers. Pete's Place could not compete with the lively atmosphere of Grayson's, but Chip and his friends liked unwinding at Pete's after work.

Pete had heard part of the conversation between his friend, Chip Hilton, and Nick Hunter, but he was too busy to pay much attention. But he wasn't too busy to overlook the steaming cup of tea left untouched by the young man seated at the counter opposite the booth. Pete followed him to the cash register to ring up the charge.

"Anything wrong with the tea?" he asked in a concerned voice.

The young man smiled. "No, not at all. The tea is fine. Just couldn't stomach the conversation in the booth, that's all. What's the guy's name who just came in? The one who was talking?"

"You mean the blond . . . the one with the short hair? That's Chip Hilton. He's a great athlete. Friend of mine. Want to meet him?"

"No, thanks. I just wondered who he was. Thanks again and good night."

Pete glanced at the booths. Nick Hunter's group was preparing to leave, and Chip and his three friends were talking quietly. He waited by the cash register until Hunter's crowd had paid their bill and then called out to Chip.

"Hey, Chip! Read in the paper you're on the starting basketball team."

"Not on the starting team, Pete. Just on the squad. There's a difference."

"Don't let him kid you," Fireball said. "He's on it!"

"He might be just on the squad now," Whitty added, "but he'll be on the starting five just as soon as he gets in shape."

Pete nodded. "You're telling me! How are *you* making out, Soapy?"

"Well, you see, it's like this, Pete. Corrigan handles the varsity, right? And Rockwell handles the freshmen and does all the scouting, right? So Corrigan says to me this afternoon, he says, 'Soapy, you go down starting Thursday and help Rockwell out.' So, bein' the good kind of a guy I am, why, I'm going, going, gone!"

Pete blinked and nodded his head. Then he nodded again. "Yeah," he said. "Yeah, I've known that for a long time. You're real gone. You're *way* out there!"

"All right, you guys," Fireball said, playfully slapping the table with his hand. "Do we eat or sit here and talk all night?"

DRIBBLING WIZARD TO START

"That's right," Soapy added, "we've got to get in before curfew. It's another one of my new responsibilities, Pete." Soapy sat up straighter in the booth.

Later, lying awake in the room he shared with Soapy in Jefferson Hall, Chip wished there was something he could do to help his best friend forget the deep hurt of that afternoon. Soapy had put up a good front, but Chip knew the hurt was there. Chip was still trying to think of a solution when he fell into a troubled sleep.

Basketball was still king on State's campus the next morning, and everyone was talking about the game with Southern. Almost everybody on campus recognized Chip now, and he tried to avoid the sports chatter, but he couldn't miss the nods in his direction and the whispered references.

"That's Hilton. They say he's better in basketball than he is in football."

"Two sports? Tough to do that."

"It's the truth. You see Monday's paper? That's what Bill Bell said."

"Well, he better be good! Southern's tough!"

"So what? State's going to the Holiday Invitational."

"Southern won the Big Twelve conference. Their whole team is back."

"Our team is good. We'll take them tonight. Especially with Hilton in the lineup. He's the best shot in the country."

Soapy met Chip in the library right after lunch and tossed a copy of the *Herald* on the table. "You see this, Chip? The story about Jimmy Chung?"

"No, I didn't. What does it say?"

"Read it."

TOURNAMENT CRISIS

STATE UNVEILS DRIBBLING STAR TONIGHT
Hardcourt Wizard to Start
by Bill Bell

Tonight at Assembly Hall, Coach Jim Corrigan will present the player he calls, "one of the greatest dribblers in the country." Although State meets Southern in a game that will have no effect upon conference standings, the contest will go a long way in determining the championship stature of the Statesmen and the athletic ability of Li Hong "Jimmy" Chung to spark a veteran team to greatness.

Jimmy Chung, returning serviceman, is not unknown to State basketball fans. Chung was on the varsity basketball squad here three years ago as a sophomore and returned this year to enter the junior class and complete his education.

Chung is an exceptional athlete. He was so highly regarded as a physics student three years ago that the army assigned him to a special group working on a classified defense project. With the project completed and his tour finished, Chung is back in school to complete his science program.

I enjoyed several conversations with various members of State's Physics Department faculty, and all enthusiastically praised Chung's science ability and predicted an impressive future for the brilliant student.

Chip tapped the paper. "That's a great article. Mind if I tear it out?"

"Of course not, but why?"

"Because it's a nice write-up."

Soapy was puzzled. "What d'ya want it for?"

"I just think it's a good story, that's all."

Soapy gave Chip a long look. "I wouldn't think you'd want any part of that show-off," he muttered gruffly.

"Soapy, did you ever stop to think how you would act if you were the only redhead with freckles trying to make a Chinese basketball team in Beijing?"

Soapy grinned. "Now there's a *real* idea! You really think I could make a Chinese basketball team? Are there transfer rules I should know? Does State have a semester-abroad program for basketball too?" He waited for the reaction. When it was evident that Chip found his attempt at humor distasteful, he sobered and meekly said, "Sorry, Chip. Guess maybe I'd act a whole lot worse than Jimmy Chung. OK?"

"Sure. Forget it. I'm going to work. Coming?"

"Good idea. Let's go."

Both boys took advantage of every chance to repay George Grayson for his generosity in scheduling their work hours to accommodate their classes and sports participation. On game days, there was no practice, so Chip and Soapy used that time to repay their kind and understanding employer.

That night, Chip was the first player to put on his uniform. He gave the laces of his left basketball shoe a final tug and leaned back against the door of his locker, acutely aware that this was the first time in a long time that he and Soapy had not suited up together. He and Speed exchanged glances, and Chip could tell that his hometown teammate was thinking the same thing.

Sky Bollinger was perched on one of the trainers' tables, and Mike Murphy was taping the big player's ankles. Sky caught Chip's glance and winked. Chip returned the wink and pushed back hard against the locker, his long fingers gripping the hard bench. This was the part that was tough. The waiting . . .

By eight o'clock everyone was in uniform. Coach Corrigan came in for his pregame talk. He waited until the players quieted. "Let me have your attention, men. One of the State traditions is the election of a captain just before the first game. So let's get at it. Here, Murph, hand out these seven pieces of paper. Lettermen only. That means everyone except the sophomores. Now let me have the nominations."

Bill King raised his hand. "Kirk Barkley," he said, grinning at Di Santis.

Di Santis came right back. "Andy Thornhill!"

"Any other nominations?" Corrigan asked. "No? All right, here's a couple of pencils. Pass 'em around."

The pencils moved around the circle, and Kelly collected the votes. Corrigan sorted them into three piles on a training table for everyone to see. One pile had only a single piece of paper while the other two had three each.

"Tie vote," Bill King whispered jubilantly. "Cocaptains!"

Corrigan verified the count. "That's right," he said. "Kirk Barkley and Andy Thornhill each have three votes. Congratulations, Kirk, Andy."

"Someone didn't vote," Barkley said accusingly. "How come?"

"Yes," Thornhill added. "Put-up job!"

Bill King nodded. "You're right!" he quipped. "I didn't vote. We happen to like both you guys."

"Time, Coach," Kelly warned, glancing at the clock.

Corrigan banged the table with the palm of his hand, and the players quieted instantly. "We'll start with Barkley and Thornhill up front, King at center, Chung and Gowdy in the backcourt. You men know as much about Southern as I do, so it's up to you. Let's go!"

Jimmy Chung was the last veteran to leave the room. He paused at the door long enough to cast a triumphant look in Chip's direction. Chip smiled and immediately forgot the incident. This was his first varsity college game, and the cheers, crowd noise, and band music thrilled him to his toes, imbuing him with an intense desire to play. He wanted to get out on the court and run Southern into the ground!

Southern was reputed to be one of the most outstanding teams in the country and proved it right from the blast of the starting whistle. The visitors worked a play off the center top so easily and smoothly that it didn't look as if they were trying. It was the old "guard down" play, one of the oldest in the game: center to forward to guard cutting down the same side of the court.

Corrigan and every player on the State bench saw the play coming and yelled, "Heads up! Chung! Jimmy! Watch out, switch!" But their shouts of warning were too late.

The Southern center outjumped King, tapped the ball to the forward Jimmy was guarding, and a speedy guard streaked down the sideline and took the pass under the basket for the tally. He scored before Jimmy Chung fully realized what had happened.

That first play set the pattern for the game. The Southerners were opportunists, taking advantage of every State mistake and keeping their own turnovers to a minimum. When State had the ball, Southern's players switched beautifully for one another and proved Southern was a defensive-minded club.

State's veterans played Corrigan's slow, methodical style of basketball using up almost every second on the shot clock. The set plays lacked color and dramatic action, but the style was good enough to keep the game close. With the exception of Jimmy Chung, who dribbled too much and shot too often, the play of the State veterans was steady, if not too effective. Chung's tricky passes often threw his receiver off balance and led to turnovers. The visitors jumped into the lead and kept it throughout the game.

Chip watched every move Chung and Gowdy made. Jimmy was by far the better offensive player, but defensively, he made a lot of serious mistakes—mistakes that cost State precious points.

Corrigan took him out late in the third quarter and replaced him with J. C. Tucker. Thereafter, the team played better defensive ball but lacked the scoring punch to keep pace with Southern.

The only other players to see much action in the dreary game were Dom Di Santis for Gowdy and Sky Bollinger for King. The final score: Southern 68, State 56.

Grayson's was the gathering spot for State University's sports fans, and many of them stopped by after the game to talk basketball. Most of the customers knew and liked Soapy, Fireball Finley, and Philip Whittemore, and the three counter employees usually had time to talk sports with the customers. But not tonight. The three athletes were hustling every second to fill orders for the hungry crowd, but they didn't miss the chatter.

"Southern was too good. What a defense!"

"We need someone who can score."

"How you going to score holding the ball for almost the entire shot clock's thirty-five seconds?"

"Got something there. Bet we didn't take fifty shots!"

"I counted fifteen passes one time before we took a shot."

"The crowd didn't like it, that's for sure."

"Same goes for the players. Bradley Gowdy's a friend of mine. He doesn't like it."

Jimmy Chung and Rodney Early came in a little later and sat down at the counter. Both were strangers to Fireball, and he wouldn't have given them a second glance except he heard the name "Chip Hilton." Fireball shot a quick glance in their direction, but they were evidently unaware he was listening.

"But Hilton *is* good. I *know*."

"Just because he can play football doesn't mean he can play basketball."

"Listen, Jimmy. I don't mean football. I'm talking basketball. Freshman basketball. He was great!"

Chung shrugged disdainfully. "Hah! Freshman basketball! That's kid stuff."

"The AAU shooting championship isn't kid stuff."

"Anyone can shoot when there's no one guarding him."

"I wish you would take my advice and play ball with him. He's a nice guy," Early insisted.

"But he isn't a basketball player. He hasn't tried a shot, and I took the ball away from him twice in a row. If that old has-been, Henry Rockwell, wasn't one of Corrigan's assistants, Hilton would have been cut from the squad with the rest of you guys."

"Have it your way, Jimmy, but don't say I didn't tell you."

When Early and Chung left the fountain and reached the cashier, Fireball pointed them out to Soapy. "You know that little guy, Soapy? The Chinese guy?"

Soapy nodded. "Sure. That's Jimmy Chung, the one that's been needling Chip. The other guy is Rodney Early. Why?"

Fireball told him about the conversation, and Soapy became livid. "That does it!" he said angrily. "Wait until I tell Chip what Chung said about the Rock. Chip won't let him get away with that!"

CHAPTER 6

Don't Knock the Rock!

JIM CORRIGAN, a young and talented coach, was ambitious and proud of his profession. He loved his job and had looked forward to a successful season. But last night's defeat had gotten to him, and the tired lines on his face reflected a sleepless night. While sitting at his desk and reading Jim Locke's story in the *News,* a frown of annoyance deepened the two little lines already etched between Corrigan's dark eyes.

STATE LOSES OPENER TO SOUTHERN
by Jim Locke

Southern spoiled State's opening game of the season last night by defeating the Statesmen, 68-56. Coach Jim Corrigan presented a veteran team and a style of basketball that was obsolete when my friends and I were playing sports in elementary school!

The only interesting feature of the game was the

performance of Jimmy Chung, who sparked
Corrigan's attack (?) during the first half and the part
of the second half he played.

Corrigan closed the paper with an angry gesture. "I'd
like to—"

"Morning, Jim. Busy?"

Corrigan looked up with annoyance that quickly vanished when Henry Rockwell entered and sat down on the
other side of the desk. Managing a grin, Corrigan tossed
the newspaper on the desk. "No, Rock, far from busy.
When did you get in?"

"Late last night. I came in on the red-eye. Too bad
about last night. What happened?"

"We couldn't score. They got out in front, and we just
couldn't catch up. How's Washington University?"

"About like we are, I'd say. They run a lot, play man
to man, and just about match us for size. I'll have the
notes ready for practice."

"Are you going to use your freshmen to demonstrate?"

"Sure! I'd like to."

Rockwell picked up the newspaper. "I see your pal is
at it again."

"He's no pal of mine," Corrigan said bitterly. "Did you
read it?"

"Yes, Jim," Rockwell said sympathetically, "I did.
Forget it. I've been down that road many times. Don't let
it get you down."

During the thoughtful silence that followed,
Corrigan studied the face of the veteran mentor.
Rockwell had retired two years ago from his job at Valley
Falls High School, where he had been coach of football,
basketball, and baseball. He then accepted a position on

State's athletic department coaching staff. *He doesn't look his age,* Corrigan was thinking. *His hair is still black, and his face hasn't got as many wrinkles as mine. He hasn't got an ounce of fat on his body either. He must be past sixty, at least. Anyway, I'm lucky to have an experienced coach like him for an assistant.*

"Rock," he said at last, "do you think he's right? Do you think we should change our style of play?"

"It's a little late for that, Jim. I think he's right about the need for a scoring punch. And as he says, our defense isn't good."

"What do you think we ought to do?"

"I think we ought to make a couple of changes."

"What changes?"

"Well, I think Hilton should be worked into the lineup as quickly as possible. He can shoot, and he's a fine defensive player. I know he's not in shape yet, but he'll come along fast. He ought to be working with the regulars and—"

"And—" Corrigan prompted.

"And I think Bollinger, Morris, and Reardon ought to see a little more action."

"Who would you bench?"

"That's a tough one, Jim." Rockwell eased himself a little lower in his chair, his eyes concentrating on an object outside the window behind Corrigan. Then he cocked an eye at the younger man and slowly smiled. "You might not like this, but if it were me, I'd bench Jimmy Chung. He's too erratic for the deliberate attack we're using. If we were using the fast break, yes, but for the slow advance and possession attack, no."

Corrigan nodded thoughtfully. "I guess you're right. He was pretty bad last night, but I figured he was just pressing, trying too hard."

"He'll never be a steady player, Jim. He has to have the ball."

"That's the trouble with most players," Corrigan agreed. "They don't know what to do *without* the ball. That's one of the reasons I use a set attack."

"You want me to scout Southwestern tomorrow night?"

"I sure do. Tomorrow *and* Saturday. I know they'll be tough on their own court, but I want to be ready for the tournament, just in case we draw them. We probably will. I see they won number thirty-eight last night."

Rockwell nodded his head, smiling ruefully. "And they ran up a big score doing it. Jeff Habley's a peculiar man. He seems to get a kick out of pouring it on a team when he's got them down."

"Not very many coaches like him, that's for sure. He has the teams though."

"He gets the players, Jim, that's all. Gets them from all over. His attack seems to be built around the big center, Bordon, and his captain, Ralk. Both made all-American last year."

"They average around thirty points apiece, don't they?"

Rockwell pulled a piece of paper out of his pocket. "That's right," he said, reading off the statistics. "Bordon averages thirty a game and Ralk twenty-eight. Then it's Perkins with twelve, Lloyd with ten, and Munn with eight. That's an eighty-eight-point average per game for the starting five, and Habley keeps them in the game right down to the wire. So he keeps the horses in and runs up the score."

"How big *are* they? I know Bordon's pushing seven feet."

"They're big enough," Rockwell said grimly. "Listen!

Bordon, six-eleven; Perkins, six-six; Ralk, six-four; Munn, six-three; Lloyd, six-two. That's an average of six-five, and knowing Habley's reputation, you can bet your life it's an understatement."

Corrigan threw up his hands. "Stop! You're scaring me to death. Let's change the subject. Do you think we can take Washington?"

"I think so. Anyway, I'll have all the stats ready by four o'clock. See you then."

Corrigan wasn't the only one upset by the newspapers that day. Soapy found Chip at the library as usual and placed a copy of the *Herald,* opened to the sports page, on the table.

"You made the paper, my friend," the redhead said lightly. "Bill Bell again!"

"Now what?"

"He says Chip Hilton would give State a scoring threat and someone to build the attack around. How do you like that?"

"I don't!"

"Guess Bill Bell doesn't care whether you like it or not. You know what else? He says Bollinger and Reardon can shoot almost as well as you can. Then he gets real tough and says that it doesn't make much sense to field an all-veteran team that isn't going anywhere and keep a bench of talented sophomores on the sidelines. Hot stuff, eh?"

"Sounds more like Jim Locke than Bill Bell."

"Maybe so, but that's what he said. Come on, it's lab time. You've got chem, and I'm off to bio. Three hours of dead fish and uncooked frog legs, and no food allowed in the labs."

DON'T KNOCK THE ROCK!

Jimmy Chung read the papers that day too. Every athlete likes to see his name in a lineup in the paper, and Jimmy was no exception. He read the account of the game in both the *News* and the *Herald,* and then he read Jim Locke's and Bill Bell's columns. When he finished Bell's column, his face was flushed with anger. "What's the matter with Bell?" he muttered. "Every day it's Hilton! He can't shoot and he can't pass, yet everyone says he's a great player just because he made all-American in football. I hope I get a chance at him this afternoon."

Jimmy Chung got his chance. Rockwell used his freshmen to present the Washington attack, defense, and out-of-bounds plays. Then he described the strong and weak points of the Washington players and demonstrated each one with individual members of his freshman squad. When he finished, Corrigan worked his regular starting five against Rockwell's squad. Then they were excused. Soapy moved up in the bleachers beside Murph Kelly to watch the varsity practice.

Down on the court, Corrigan was talking. "We'll have a thirty-minute scrimmage and call it a day. Starting team as is, and let's have Bollinger, Hilton, Di Santis, Tucker, and Slater out here to start."

The teams lined up, and Jimmy once again sought out and paired up against Chip. Soapy grunted in anticipation and nudged Kelly. "Watch this," he whispered. "Watch Chip."

"What's up?" Kelly asked.

"Just watch!"

Bollinger used the previous year's freshman jump signal, and Chip came in high, got the tap, and handed off to Tucker. Tucker hit Di Santis, and the big man zipped the ball back to Chip in the backcourt. As soon as

Chip caught the ball, Jimmy dove forward and tried to knock the ball out of his hand. Then the little dribbler got a surprise. Chip jerked the ball back out of range and went around Chung as if the dribbler were nailed to the floor.

Before one of Jimmy's teammates could switch to cover him, Chip stopped at the head of the free-throw circle and used his jumper. The ball swished through the basket for the two-pointer without touching the rim.

Chung was seething. "Lucky," he gritted. "Lucky shot."

Chip smiled and covered Jimmy like snow on the Matterhorn, and his opponent was forced to pass. And when Chung reversed his direction so he would be in position to regain the ball, Chip dropped carelessly back and turned his head to watch the ball.

Up in the bleachers, Soapy nudged Murph Kelly again. "Watch!"

"I'm watching!" Kelly growled. "Quit jabbing me, Soapy!"

When Gowdy returned the pass, Chip erupted into action, intercepted the ball, and was away with Chung in swift pursuit. Chip drove under the basket and faked, and Jimmy flew through the air in anticipation of the shot. At the last instant, Chip drew the ball back, watched Chung fly past him and out of bounds, and then calmly reached up and banked the ball off the backboard and through the ring.

Jimmy took the ball out of bounds and passed it to Gowdy, who brought the ball slowly upcourt. Jimmy could scarcely wait for the ball, but Gowdy passed to Barkley, and the cocaptain hit Bill King under the basket. The big senior hooked cleanly over Sky Bollinger's outstretched arm, and the ball dropped through the hoop.

DON'T KNOCK THE ROCK!

Sky caught the ball as it dropped through the cords; he then stepped back out of bounds. Next he rifled a pass to Rudy Slater halfway up the court. Rudy dribbled hard for the basket, but Barkley cut him off, so Rudy passed back to Chip near the center of the court.

Chip held the ball at arm's length over his head and looped a high pass to Bollinger. Sky met the ball on the side of the lane, and Chip ran Jimmy into the block and cut through. But Bill King saw the play coming. He yelled, "Switch!," and picked Chip up as he drove past.

Chung switched back when Chip didn't get the ball, and Bollinger dribbled to the corner. Sky held the ball until Chip maneuvered to a pivot position by the side of the basket, just outside the three-second lane. Then he gave Chip a perfect bounce pass. The rest was easy. Chip faked, drew the foul, and went right on up with the shot to score. He tossed the free throw cleanly through the net to complete the three-point play and dropped back on defense, feeling loose for the first time.

Chung was wary now. And the next time Chip got the ball, the little dribbler gave Chip plenty of room. Chip gauged the distance to the goal, faked a dribble, took a long step back, and let the ball fly. The shot never touched the rim.

Soapy elbowed Murph Kelly nearly out of his seat. "You see that?" he demanded gleefully.

"I saw it, all right, and I like it," Kelly answered. "But remember my age. I bruise easily. What fired Hilton up?"

"Jimmy Chung said some things he shouldn't have said about a member of the coaching staff. Guess this will take care of *him*."

Kelly grinned. "Hope so. He had it coming."

After Chip's last shot, Corrigan substituted Speed Morris for Tucker and Reardon for Chip. Then he moved

Chip over to the starting five in place of Chung. Chip had no difficulty blending in with the regulars, and following a short scrimmage, Corrigan excused the squad for the day.

When Chip and Speed came out of Assembly Hall, Soapy was waiting, barely able to control his jubilation. "Nice going, Chipper. That was great!"

"It was a cheap thing to do," Chip said bitterly, ashamed of himself.

"Why?"

"Because it wasn't a fair match."

"But he asked for it, Chip. Look what he did to you! What's the difference?"

"I thought we settled that Wednesday."

"You mean about me and Beijing?"

"That's right," Chip said shortly. "Now forget it."

About the same time, in another area near the campus, Jimmy Chung was slowly walking home to his small, off-campus apartment. He was in a thoughtful frame of mind and thoroughly mixed up about a lot of things. There was, first of all, his shaky position as a starting guard on the varsity; second, his poor play and removal from the game the previous night; and third, the emergence this afternoon of Chip Hilton as a dangerous competitor for his position.

Jimmy tried to tell himself that Hilton had just been lucky that afternoon. But he knew deep in his heart that an athlete with Hilton's speed and passing and shooting ability, as demonstrated in the afternoon scrimmage, was no ordinary player. "Rodney was right," he muttered. "He's good. Now I *am* in for a tough time."

CHAPTER 7

The Golden Rule

HENRY ROCKWELL was only partly right about Washington University. The two teams were evenly matched in height, and both teams used man-to-man defense, but that's where the comparison ended. Washington's attack sparkled; State's offense sputtered.

Corrigan started Barkley, King, Thornhill, Gowdy, and Tucker. And when this team failed to click, he began to experiment with different veteran combinations. Consequently, the starters and reserve veterans lost their confidence, and the outcome was bad basketball. Washington gradually forged ahead and led by a score of 42-30 at the half. The beginning of the second half was a repetition of the first, and when Corrigan called time with ten minutes left, Washington was still ahead by twelve points: 61-49.

Corrigan pulled all his veterans out and replaced them with Chip, Sky Bollinger, Speed Morris, Rudy Slater, and Bitsy Reardon. "All right, men," he said, glancing at the scoreboard, "we're down twelve points, so we haven't got a thing to lose. Play them all over the court but watch the fouls. And another thing, switch on every cross. Got it? OK, now go get 'em!"

The sophomores gave all they had and fought Washington to a standstill. Their spirit and drive were so exciting after the dull play of the veterans that the State fans took heart. But it was too much to ask as the sophomores hadn't been together as a team since the previous year. Washington had too much poise, lasted it out, and won 82-75.

By the time Chip and Speed finished dressing, it was too late to go to work. They walked slowly across the campus to Jeff. On the way, they talked over the game.

"We nearly caught them," Speed said ruefully.

Chip nodded. "I've been thinking about that. You know, if we'd had Jimmy Chung in the game instead of Rudy, we might have done it. He's fast, has wonderful reflexes, and loves a wide-open game. He's a natural for a press attack."

"You're right. I never thought of him that way."

"It wouldn't be bad," Chip continued. "Sky is big and fast, Bitsy is a flash of lightning, and you're as fast as they come. Hmmm."

"No one could say you had two left feet," Speed added. "I wish Corrigan would work us as a team."

By that time the two athletes, friends since elementary school, had reached Jeff and slowly climbed the stairs to their rooms on the second floor.

Chip smiled at Speed. "We can think about it and be ready the next time. Let's keep thinking about it. Well, I've got to get some sleep. See you in the morning."

Down at Grayson's, interest in the game had been high. In between serving customers, Soapy's eyes were glued to the big-screen TV. When he had to serve someone, his eyes left the screen only long enough to be sure the ice cream was securely perched atop the cone or that the burger had really landed on the bun. His whole being swelled with pride as he watched his hometown friends, Speed Morris and Chip Hilton, finally get into the game. And his heart leaped with each basket as Chip racked up sixteen points in ten minutes.

When Soapy got home, Chip was asleep. The redhead undressed quietly and went to bed. In the morning, he shook Chip awake.

"Locke is on Corrigan's case, Chip. Listen! And I quote:

"'Now, I could be wrong, but it was always my understanding that the game of basketball is won by the team that puts the ball through the hoop more often than its opponents.

"'Last night at Assembly Hall, Washington University won a dull contest by a score of 82-75, chiefly because the locals handled the ball as if it were a rare dinosaur egg, and they were afraid to shoot it because it might break.

"'Speaking of dinosaurs, this careful ballhandling was supposed to demonstrate Corrigan's famous possession-passing attack, but its only effect on some twelve thousand fans was to send them away from the game with little to remember about a wasted evening except that they had been first-hand witnesses to a first-class sports bust.

"'The only spark of life was provided by Chip Hilton, a sophomore up from last year's freshman team, who scored sixteen points during the ten minutes he was in the game. Hilton averaged thirty-four points per game as a freshman, and that's probably why Corrigan kept him on the bench.'

"And listen to this, Chip. 'Southwestern won its thirty-ninth-straight game last night. As usual, Bordon and Ralk led the way: Bordon under the basket with his sensational hooks and tap-ins, and Ralk with his three-pointers.'"

"Thirty-nine in a row." Chip expelled a deep breath in appreciation. "What a record! I'd be proud just to sit the bench on a team like that."

"Don't worry, you'd have a starting spot. C'mon. I'm starved."

After breakfast, Chip and Soapy hustled down to Grayson's and worked steadily through the day. Chip was thinking ahead to the game that night. The hours slipped away like minutes, and then he was in the locker room and Corrigan was pacing back and forth in front of the team, giving his pregame talk.

"We learned a lot last night, and I know we're not going to let Washington beat us two nights in succession. Let's go out there and play *real* basketball."

State did, all right! The Statesmen jumped into the lead after a ragged start by both teams and remained out in front during the entire game. Chip got a chance in parts of both halves and was sensational, scoring twenty-nine points and bringing the fans to their feet time after time with his accurate shooting.

"You see that? You see that shot?"

"They can't hold him! I never saw anything like it!"

"*How* can Corrigan keep *him* off the starting five?"

Jimmy Chung was bitterly disappointed, and it showed in his behavior on the bench. He pouted and sat with folded arms, never once joining his bench team-mates in cheering a good play on the court. Corrigan seemed to have forgotten all about the dribbling wizard and did not give him a chance until there were only three minutes left to play.

As soon as he was in the game, and the first time he got his hands on the ball, Jimmy dribbled in for a shot. Chip followed in, got the ball, passed it back to Chung, and maneuvered his opponent into a pick. When he broke for the basket, there were six feet of daylight between himself and his guard, but Chung passed him up and held the ball. Before there was time for another shot, the game was over.

The locker room was full of chatter and horseplay, but Jimmy Chung did not join in the fun. He was still upset. He banged his shoes and uniform into his locker and slammed the metal door. On the way out of the building, Chip found himself walking beside Jimmy and tried to cheer him up. "Don't worry about it, Jimmy. You'll be back in there. Coach is just trying everyone out."

Chung shrugged his shoulders and glared at Chip without a word. At the first corner he turned and strode away without responding to Chip's "Good night."

A few minutes later Jimmy was in one of the science labs on campus with George Long, one of his school friends and a graduate assistant.

"What happened?" Long asked, gesturing toward the radio as he worked. "Why didn't you play?"

Jimmy threw himself down on a chair. "Too many big-shot football stars out for the team."

"That guy Hilton was terrific. Got twenty-nine points. He was high scorer of the game."

"I hate that kid," Chung said angrily. "The jerk!" Then, noting the expression on Long's face, he reflected a second and added lamely, "Maybe I don't hate him, but—man, I don't know how I feel about him."

"I know how *I* feel about him!"

Chung was surprised. "You know him?"

"Not personally, but I know him well enough to tell you that you're wrong about the jerk business. He's anything *but!* I happen to know! And no matter how you feel about his basketball ability, Jimmy, he's going to be the star of the team."

"What do you mean, you know him?"

"I know he's a gentleman. Have you ever been in Pete's Place? That little restaurant on Tenth Street?"

"Don't think so. Why?"

"Well, I went in there for a cup of tea the other night, and some students were sitting in a booth talking basketball. Naturally, knowing you, I listened in. Then Hilton and somebody called Soapy came in, and one of the guys in the booth spoke to this Soapy and said he was glad he'd been cut from the squad because he didn't care to play on the same team with a foreigner."

Jimmy Chung shook his head. "Yeah, so? I don't get it."

"He meant *you*," Long continued. "He called you by name."

"But I'm not a foreigner. I'm a Chinese-American. But what's that got to do with Hilton?"

"Plenty! Hilton told him off! He said you were born of naturalized parents and were as much a citizen or an American as he or anyone else. Hilton really shut him up!"

"You're not kidding? He really did that? Stood up for me?"

"He sure did."

There was a short, tense silence. Then Jimmy Chung struck the table with his fist, jarring test tubes and rattling bottles. "Guess *I'm* the jerk!" he said in disgust. "I wonder when I'll really grow up. I've sure been wrong about him."

Jimmy reflected a moment, nodding his head thoughtfully. Then he eyed his friend steadily and continued. "You're right about the basketball part of it, too, George. He's a great player."

After Jimmy Chung had walked away, Chip had continued toward Grayson's and a few minutes later joined Soapy, Fireball, and Whitty at Pete's. Pete greeted Chip warmly. "What happened to you last night? Missed you. You hear what Gee-Gee Gray had to say about you on his sportscast? Your ears burn last night?"

Chip grinned. "No, but maybe that's why I had some bad dreams."

"Uh-uh. It was all good. You stick around. It will be better tonight. Mentioning bad dreams, I was so tired last night when I got to bed I couldn't even sleep. This place has been mobbed for the past week."

Soapy elbowed Pete. "Why don't you break down and hire some help?" he gibed.

"You ever try hiring restaurant help? They last about a week, and then they're gone and you look again. Seriously, though, if you know of someone who wants a job, send him around. But he's gotta have experience. I ain't got time to teach a guy how to carry a glass of water without spilling it."

Chip's friends wanted to know all about the game, so he had to replay it for them. He was glad when they reached Jeff and he could get to bed. He was always dead tired when Sunday rolled around, and he looked forward to a good, long, late sleep.

But not Soapy Smith. Soapy was always wide awake at the crack of dawn. And Sunday was no exception. He slipped quietly out of the room and went for the papers. Chip was half awake when Soapy returned, but that meant little to Soapy. He tugged at Chip's sheets to gain his attention, opened the paper with a sharp rattle to the sports page, and then threw himself down on his bed.

"Listen to this quote, Chip. 'After two straight defeats, State got into the winning column last night at Assembly Hall, defeating Washington 79-64 to break even in the two-game series. . . . Chip Hilton proved to be the big gun for the Statesmen, scoring twenty-nine points in just over twenty minutes of play.'"

"Please, Soapy, I know all this," Chip protested. "I was there, remember?"

Unfazed, Soapy came right back. "OK, how about this? Quote: 'Southwestern won its fortieth consecutive victory last night and appeared unbeatable. Coach Jeff Habley's NCAA and Holiday Invitational champions brushed aside Southern Poly 109-64 with all-American "Two-Ton" Tom Bordon scoring thirty-two points and hogging twenty-six rebounds. His teammate, all-American Reggie "Allnet" Ralk, scored twenty-nine points during the eighteen minutes he saw action.' Wow, Chip! How about those guys?"

"Fabulous, that's all. Well, I suppose you're happy now that you've got me wide awake," Chip muttered half seriously, half to tease Soapy. "But remember this, when I get back from church, I'm going to take a long nap. Then I'm going to study. All day! Understand?"

"Have no fears, my famous friend. I've got a little errand that concerns Miss Mitzi Savrill, and it will keep me busy all day, starting as of now. See you at lunch."

Chip showered and dressed, ate breakfast at the student union, and started for church. He had taken fewer than ten steps when he passed a figure who was slouching with his head lowered and his hands thrust deep in his pockets, evidently deep in thought. Chip glanced at the walker and was surprised to see that it was Jimmy Chung.

"Hey, Jimmy. Going anywhere in particular?"

Chung, startled out of his reverie, jumped. He recovered his poise quickly and shook his head. "Uh, no, Hilton. Just taking a walk."

"If you're not doing anything, how about going along to church with me?"

Jimmy was surprised. His eyes opened a bit wider, and he stared quizzically at Chip. "Sure." He paused and looked at his clothes. "I—"

"You look all right. Come on."

They matched strides for a few steps, each feeling a little uncomfortable. Jimmy was the first to speak. "You know something, Hilton?"

"Call me Chip."

"Chip, then. You're the first guy on the squad who has really been friendly. And I've been too much of a chump to realize it."

"Hey, they think you're great, Jimmy!"

"No, it's something else. They laugh at my act, but they don't really like me. I guess it's because I'm such a show-off."

"You're wrong. Everyone likes you. Well, here we are."

Chip and Jimmy sat quietly through the church service, and an hour later when they walked slowly down the steps with the other worshipers, each realized he had found a friend.

"What did you think of the sermon?" Chip asked.

"We worship a little differently, Chip, but I thought it was really good. The whole time the minister was talking, I was thinking about sports. Seems to me sportsmanship in almost anything an athlete does is on the religious side."

"No doubt about it, Jimmy. The Golden Rule just about covers everything: 'Do unto others as you would have others do unto you.'"

Jimmy nodded. "Yes," he agreed thoughtfully, "that *would* cover about everything."

They continued along in silence, and then Chip put his thoughts into words. "Jimmy, I'd like to be your friend, and I'd like you to be my friend. But there's something wrong."

"Nothing is wrong, Chip," Jimmy said slowly. "Nothing, that is, except me. I love basketball, and my heart is set on making the first team. It means more to me right now than almost anything else in the world."

He shrugged his shoulders and spread his hands. "I guess I might just as well say it. I was trying to show you up because I realized how good you were and was afraid you would beat me out for the team.

"I'm from Springfield, Chip, and I've been hoping I could start against Wilson University in my hometown. We go out there on the fifteenth, and if I can play in that game, well, everything in my little world will be tops. That is, except—"

"Except what?"

"Well, I've got to have a job and quick. I've already asked about working at the science department, and there's going to be a job available next term. I was hoping I could hang on this semester and wait for the science job, but I need to work now."

"I thought your books and tuition were covered from being in the army."

"They are. But unfortunately, every penny I can

spare has to go home to help my family. Things are pretty serious with my pop's business right now."

"What sort of work are you looking for?"

"Well, if I can't do something in science, a restaurant's the next thing I know the most about. Guess I ought to know the restaurant business," Jimmy said glumly. "I've worked in one just about all my life. That's our business in Springfield." His voice grew tight. "Not that there's much business—"

Chip stopped him short and snapped his fingers. "All right! I know where you can get a job. What are you doing tomorrow after practice?"

"Nothing. That's the trouble."

"Good. I've got an idea, and I'm going to put it to work right now. I'll tell you about it tomorrow at practice."

CHAPTER 8

Filial Piety

CHIP HEADED straight for Pete's Place, his spirits high and his long legs rapidly eating up the distance. Soapy was absorbed with a crossword puzzle in one of the booths lining the wall opposite the counter. Chip slid into the seat opposite the redhead.

"English assignment?" Chip grinned.

Soapy shook his head. "Real funny," he growled. "I'm just trying to win a trip to China! I want to learn how to dribble a basketball!"

"Soapy—"

"I was just kidding," Soapy grinned disarmingly and winked at Pete, who had approached the booth. "Gimme another hamburger and a milk shake, eh, Pete?"

Pete grimaced. "It's your stomach." He leaned against the side of the booth and turned to Chip. "What can I do for *you,* Chip?"

"Oh, a grilled cheese with tomato and a glass of milk, I guess. Pete, that job you spoke about still open?"

"Sure is. Know somebody?"

"I think so. He's had restaurant experience and needs a job."

"A student?"

"Yes. He's a student here at State. He's Chinese-American and a good person."

Soapy's head shot up, and he looked at Chip in astonishment. "Chinese-American," he repeated.

"How about the language?" Pete asked.

"Speaks better English than either of us."

Pete hesitated. "I don't know, Chip. Some pretty rough guys hang out in here." His quick glance caught the disappointment in Chip's eyes. He added quickly, "But for you, anything! Bring him around."

"There's one more thing, Pete. He's a great basketball player. He's on the team."

Pete's face lit up. "He is? Now *that's* an interesting aspect." He eyed Chip keenly, nodding his head understandingly. "Uh-*huh!* And you want me to arrange his hours so he can practice and play games. That's easy enough! Fact is, it oughta help business. Fancy me having a varsity basketball player working in my restaurant. Just like Grayson's! Sure he can get off. Anytime!"

When Chip and Soapy finished eating and had paid their bill, Pete told Chip he would be expecting his new employee the next afternoon. "Thanks, Chip," he said appreciatively.

Once outside Pete's Place, Soapy, who was bursting with curiosity, spluttered, "What's that all about? Why are you getting Jimmy Chung a job?"

"Because he needs one."

"How do you know?"

Chip told Soapy about taking Jimmy to church and

their talk. "He's all right, Soapy. He's lonely and he needs friends. Jimmy feels he's disliked."

Soapy grunted. "Well, he's got that right! What an attitude! I sure hope all Chinese-Americans aren't show-offs like him. Hey, you've been studying Chinese history in that course with Dr. Kennedy. Are all Chinese people like Jimmy Chung?"

"I don't know, Soapy. Are all redheads comics? Or only the ones with freckles?"

"OK, Chip, I get your point." Soapy reddened, his freckles becoming even more prominent with his blush.

"Of course, Dr. Kennedy does say that the Chinese have a long history, great perseverance in overcoming obstacles and adversity, and strong family ties. And you have to admit Jimmy is persevering."

"He's that, all right. Especially when it comes to dribbling."

"He paid a price for that, Soapy. Dr. Kennedy keeps pounding the Chinese perseverance element into us. One of his favorite Chinese axioms is: 'The sea was great; the bird small. The bird picked up stones and dropped them into the sea until the sea was filled.'"

"All right, that's persevering. So what?"

"It's more than that. . . . They're strong and intense and they never give up. They've lost wars, too, but the Chinese have never surrendered their souls or ideals."

"All right," Soapy agreed grudgingly, "they're clever and persevering and strong and have high ideals. I hope all this means your new buddy will do an about-face and try to be a regular guy."

"He will. Come on. I've got to hit the books and send some E-mails. Think I'll call home too."

Monday's papers played up the coming game at

Southwestern on Wednesday night. But it was all about Southwestern. The writers cited all sorts of statistics covering the forty-game winning streak and the twin championships of the previous season: the Holiday Invitational Tournament and the NCAA championship. Yet even with all the coverage provided by the sportswriters, Henry Rockwell gave State's varsity some inside information on Southwestern that could scarcely have been provided by Coach Jeff Habley himself.

Rockwell had his freshman team all set by the time the varsity appeared and plunged right into the scouting notes he and Soapy had prepared. As he explained the type of attack and defense Southwestern used, his players demonstrated the moves on the court. Then Rockwell discussed each Southwestern player in detail.

"Bordon averages around thirty points a game. He's listed as six-eleven, but it's my guess he's seven feet in height or better. And don't be fooled by his weight. The program says he weighs 260 pounds, and I believe it. He isn't called 'Two-Ton' for nothing. But that doesn't mean he can't use it. He's strong and rough and he's been around. Watch his elbows, you centers. He's extremely liberal and will let you have one at any time."

That brought a laugh, but it died away as the players caught the grim undercurrent in Rockwell's voice.

"Bordon is good. But if I were to choose their key player, it would have to be Reggie Ralk. Ralk is six-four, weighs about 210, and is good for twenty-five or thirty points a game. He scores chiefly on three-pointers from the corner and gets some tip-in plays since he's always up on the boards. Now this may sound impossible, but it's another tribute to his greatness. He's smart enough and fast enough to cover the boards *and* direct the attack and the defense.

"The other big man is Perkins. He plays the corners on the offense and sets the picks and blocks for the cutters. On the defense he plays the opponents' second big man." A brief smile whisked across Rockwell's lips as he continued. "At the guard positions they have a couple of little fellows: Jim Lloyd and Joe Munn. Lloyd is six-two, 185 pounds, and gets about ten points a game. Munn is about the same size. They're both steady players and make few mistakes.

"Coach Jeff Habley plays those five players all the way. Not that he hasn't got good reserves, but Habley believes his starting five should carry the load.

"Now, I hesitate to say this, but Coach Corrigan and I both think it's only fair to warn you: Southwestern plays rough, tough, and what I would call unnecessarily bruising basketball. The players throw their elbows around carelessly and are experts at double-teaming an opposing rebounder with the kind of body contact that— shall I say—leaves a memory?

"The three big men are especially expert in the use of their hips when players try to drive through, and you can expect a shove in the back if you're in the way. Oh, yes. I might add that they are exceptionally clever. You've all heard about legendary officials who have eyes in the back of their heads. Well," Rockwell paused and continued dryly, "they wouldn't be good enough!"

After Rockwell finished sharing his notes, Corrigan scrimmaged the squad right through the full hour that remained. Chip and Jimmy dressed quickly and hurried down to Pete's Place. After the introductions, Pete put Jimmy right to work.

Soapy was behind the Grayson's fountain when Chip came in through the Tenth Street entrance. "Everything all right?" he asked.

Chip nodded. "He's already on the job."

The evening rush tapered off at nine o'clock, and Chip slipped out the side door and down the block to Pete's Place. Pete was serving coffee to one of the customers who sat at the counter, but Jimmy was nowhere in sight. When Pete finished with the customer, he hurried up to Chip, his face wreathed in smiles.

"Lookin' for Jimmy? He's in the kitchen. Know what he's doing? He's reorganizing the place. He said our efficiency could be improved with a few changes, so he's done a little rearranging, and after that he did some cleaning. You could eat off the floor in the kitchen! Whew, can that guy work! He's a human dynamo. Not only that, he's better on a quick order than the chef himself."

"The customers like him?"

"Like him? They think he's great! He's got them practically eating out of his hand."

"Tell him I'll be back after work."

"Right, Chip. He'll be here."

Soapy, Fireball, and Whitty had no curfew and could take their time after work, but not Chip and Jimmy. Chip watched the clock and started for Pete's Place just before closing time. Jimmy was waiting, and together they walked slowly up the street.

"Oh, man," Jimmy groaned, "am I tired!"

"How did it go?"

"Good, Chip. I like to be busy doing a lot of different tasks, and Pete's Place sure fills that need. I wish Pop's restaurant was that busy. Maybe I wouldn't have to worry."

"What's wrong with your father's restaurant?"

Jimmy was a little reluctant to talk about it at first, but after a few more minutes in Chip's company, he began to open up. Jimmy loved and admired his father but felt he was too tied to his ancestral customs to make his business successful in the United States. "Pop tries to run the business as if he were still in the village he grew up in near Guilin. He can't seem to understand that Americans expect service and modern surroundings."

"Lots of Americans like international restaurants, Jimmy. Everybody likes Chinese food. There are several Chinese restaurants right here in University."

"I know, Chip, but you can read their menus, can't you?"

Chip frowned. "I don't know what you mean, Jimmy."

"Pop's menus are entirely in Mandarin. He caters to the small Chinese community in Springfield. Of course they have no problem reading the menu, but it's completely useless to everybody else. Pop says serving the Chinese community is enough. Well, it's not enough to even pay the bills, and Pop's too stubborn to change from the old ways. The food is great, and our restaurant is practically on the Wilson campus! But hardly anyone outside of the Chinese community knows the restaurant is open. Pop could make a fortune if he would just cater a little to the college kids and other residents of Springfield.

"That's the reason my brother Tommy left. He didn't think it made sense to keep the restaurant open all day when there were no customers and then try to make ends meet by serving tea and expensive dishes at night to twenty or thirty people. Especially when it meant losing money. He tried to talk Pop into a takeout menu—college kids would really like that, especially if it was written in a language they could read!"

"What's Tommy doing now?" Chip asked.

Jimmy grinned. "Just what you would expect; he's working in a successful restaurant in Chicago."

"You and Tommy seem to think alike. Couldn't you team up and change your father's point of view?"

"No, Chip, you don't understand. In our way of life, the eldest son—" Jimmy paused and tapped his chest. "That's me. The eldest son is treated like a man and has to follow his father's orders to the letter. His father never shows affection for him, and it's tough. Especially when you've grown up in America and your father keeps stressing the virtues of filial piety.

"You'd call them responsibilities. *Your* responsibilities to *your* family, and to *your* ways and customs, are something like ours, with the exception that the eldest son of a Chinese family is trained from infancy to observe them to the letter. I've always tried to do that, Chip, out of reverence for my father and mother."

"What's wrong with that, Jimmy? I think that's right."

"It is, Chip, up to a certain point. But Pop is always talking about going back to China, saying how vital and important it is to us. But I feel that I am an American, and I *never* want to go back to China to live. This is my home. But you see, the old Chinese feel that the village of their birth is the most beloved spot on earth."

"Has your father been back to China?"

"Sure, years ago. You see, my grandfather was able to send Pop over here as a student, but he didn't have enough money and had to go to work instead. Anyway, he saved his money, went back home to China, married my mother, and brought her here. All of us kids were born in America, but Pop dreams about going back to his birthplace to live when we've saved enough money."

"But you're an American, and your whole family is American. Why go back?"

"Lots of the old people want to go back, Chip. They just can't believe anything over there has changed."

Jimmy shook his head firmly. "I never want to leave America. I love this country, and I want to live here until I die."

"Well, you can, can't you?"

"Yes and no. It's hard to explain. I'm a Chinese-American, Chip. But filial piety, loyalty to family, is a matter of honor and duty. And I'm the first son, so that puts the responsibility on me to care for my parents. I love my family with all my heart, and obedience to one's elders is one of our most precious beliefs. That's where the responsibilities of an American male differ from the virtues as practiced by a Chinese male. I guess you've been reading all that in your Chinese history class I've heard you mention. At any rate, it's a matter of obedience and duty. So—"

"How many are in your family, Jimmy?"

Jimmy counted on his fingers. "There's my mother, and Tommy—he's twenty years old—the four girls, my father, and my grandfather. My grandfather is old and not very active in things. But my pop tries to make the whole family think *his* way. But it just won't work. Tommy thinks American, period! So . . . he's in Chicago, and Pop never even mentions his name at home anymore. But, as you know, I'm the eldest son, and, well, I must do as Pop says."

"Maybe everything will change when you get out of college, Jimmy," Chip said. "You'll be older and able to do a lot of things for your family."

"I hope you're right," Jimmy said softly. "Well, here's where I turn off. I guess I'd better go home. I'm tired, but it's a good tired. 'Night, Chip, and thanks for the job and everything."

Practice the next day continued where it had left off the previous afternoon. Rockwell and his freshman squad again demonstrated the kind of basketball State could expect from Southwestern, and then Corrigan put the varsity through another fast scrimmage. When Chip and Jimmy came out of the gym, they found Soapy waiting.

Jimmy had recognized how Soapy felt about him and was immediately on his guard. But it wasn't necessary. The new Jimmy Chung was good enough for Soapy Smith. If Chip thought Jimmy was all right, Soapy thought he was all right too.

"Well, now that you know what you're going to be up against, what are you planning to do about it?" Soapy demanded.

"Take it as it comes and try to win," Chip replied.

"Well, you better get a good rest. You're in for a rough time tomorrow night."

Jimmy looked doubtful. "They couldn't play that way and get away with it, could they?"

"Yes, sir!" Soapy said convincingly. "If the Rock says they play that kind of basketball, that's the way they play!"

CHAPTER 9

"The Treatment"

HAWTHORN LOOKED just like any other medium-sized city from the air as the plane carrying the State University basketball team made its final approach. Players looked out the small windows to view the dotted landscape below. Scattered farms dusted with snow gave way to houses settled closer together until smaller and more residential areas filled their view. In the distance, the usual industrial buildings and small to medium-sized factories carried out their daily activities. From the air Chip marveled at the maze of interconnected highways and streets filled with cars, trucks, and bright yellow school buses making their afternoon runs.

Dressed in their traveling clothes—khaki slacks, white shirts with red and blue ties, and blue sport coats—State's varsity basketball team was an impressive sight as the players moved through the concourse to the baggage claim area. Most of the basketball players had lost interest in the scenery as soon as the plane touched down and taxied to the jetway. It was afternoon, and they were interested only in food. "When do we eat?" they cried, grabbing their individual blue and red team bags from the baggage carousel.

As they passed the gift shop, Chip glanced at the newspaper headline stretching across the top of the page in big block letters.

SOUTHWESTERN SEEKS VICTORY NUMBER 41

"It's the front-page headline!" Jimmy exclaimed in disbelief. "This place must be hoop crazy, or else nothing ever happens around here!"

Then the "treatment" began as they made their way out to the bus that was stopped at the curb.

Two businessmen entering the terminal couldn't resist a quick dig at the State team as one called, "Hey! You guys from State? Well, take our advice, get back on the plane!"

Coach Jim Corrigan had always stressed the importance of being polite as the team represented State University, but the players were also expected to remember why they were traveling and focus on the game. Kirk Barkley, Andy Thornhill, Jimmy Chung, and Chip, who were the last four players out of the terminal, ignored the man's comments and stowed their bags in the bus luggage compartment before finding empty seats. Then they got some more of the treatment as the bus made its way toward Southwestern's campus.

"Take a look!" Andre Gilbert pointed to the storefronts. Every store along the street had a big 41 painted on the windows.

"*Now* I've seen everything!" Jimmy said.

The campus was hoop crazy too. Students on the

walkways stopped, stared, and greeted them with good-natured hoots and jeers as the bus passed. It was no different as they passed buildings on the campus. Signs covered the walls that offered condolences and advice to the "next victims."

"Take it serious, don't they?" Barkley observed.

"Ignore it," Thornhill said shortly.

The bus pulled to a stop in front of Southwestern University Arena. The players lumbered off the bus and began stretching out the kinks they had from sitting in the small seats before grabbing their gear for shooting practice and a walk-through of their offense.

State's Assembly Hall was beautiful, but it couldn't compare to this elaborate structure. The giant lobby seemed as big as a football field and was lined with row upon row of trophy cases containing hundreds of game balls and sparkling trophies. Most prominently displayed were three NCAA championship plaques and two Holiday Invitational Tournament championship awards in the shape of basketballs made by Waterford Crystal in Ireland.

Chip walked through a lobby door and found himself on the mezzanine above the basketball court. He walked down to one of the boxes and viewed the shiny court below. It looked almost like a painting. "It's beautiful," he murmured aloud.

"You can say that again," someone behind him agreed.

As soon as Chip turned, he knew the middle-aged man who extended his hand was a sportswriter.

"Hello. You must be Chip Hilton. My name's Bill Gary, of the *Chronicle*. I recognized you from your picture. I ran it in the paper today. You like our court?"

"I've never seen anything like it."

"THE TREATMENT"

"You've never seen anything like our team either. We've got some of the greatest players the game has ever seen." He appraised Chip's broad, sloping shoulders and big hands. "You must be pretty good yourself. Unusual for a sophomore football player to crack the varsity basketball team."

"I guess you could call it luck."

"That isn't what I hear. Follow me. I'll walk you down to the visitor's locker room."

Bill Gary knew Jim Corrigan and stopped to chat with him, and Chip joined his teammates and slipped into his uniform. When he walked out on the highly polished floor, he found himself on tiptoe, stepping gingerly, as though he were walking on a mirror.

Corrigan held shooting practice for half an hour and then walked the players through the offense before excusing them with a reminder that the pregame meal would be served at five o'clock sharp.

After the team checked into the Southwestern Inn, Chip opened the *Chronicle* to the sports page. More of the "treatment" jumped out at him.

LOCALS READY FOR VICTIM 41
Visitors to Start Football Star

State arrived in town to meet Southwestern's NCAA basketball champions tonight at the Southwestern University Arena and is slated to be victim number 41. The visitors lost their first two games but bounced back against Washington University last Saturday night to break into the victory column with a score of 79-64.

Chip Hilton, National AAU Basketball Marksmanship Champion and State's all-American sophomore football quarterback star, scored 29 points against Washington and is expected to spearhead the attack of the Statesmen against SW tonight.

PROBABLE STARTING LINEUPS

Southwestern	State
F Ralk 42 Sr. 6-4	F Barkley 33 Sr. 6-4
F Perkins 51 Sr. 6-6	F Thornhill 51 Sr. 6-2
C Bordon 33 Sr. 6-11	C King 53 Jr. 6-9
G Lloyd 14 Jr. 6-2	G Hilton 44 So. 6-4
G Munn 23 Sr. 6-3	G Gowdy 15 Sr. 6-4

Chip glanced quickly at Jimmy, who was sitting nearby, and then folded the paper. "How about a walk?" he suggested. "Let's take a look at the campus."

It was four o'clock when they returned, and after the team meal, it was time for everyone to relax in their rooms. Chip wanted to take a nap but couldn't sleep, so he, Jimmy, and Speed rested and talked a bit about the Southwestern team as ESPN programs rolled across the TV screen unnoticed.

A preliminary game was in progress when State arrived at the arena that night, and the Statesmen watched the action until the end of the half. When they left to dress, every seat in the big arena was filled.

Corrigan wasted no time on a pregame pep talk. The treatment had taken care of him and the players as well. He merely joined in the team clasp and said, "Give 'em all you've got!"

Chip followed Barkley and Thornhill in the line of players and expected to hear a round of welcoming applause from the fans when they ran out on the floor. But there was hardly a sound. State went right into the usual warm-up routine, the players feeling a bit angry at the continuation of the treatment that had dogged them every step since their arrival at the airport.

Then, without warning, they got another dose. A siren shrilled and wailed piercingly through the great arena. The murmuring crowd noise died away until the only sound was the padding feet of the State players and the thump of the ball. Then the lights flickered out.

Surprised by the darkness and the strange silence of the crowd, Chip and his teammates looked around the pale circle of faces.

"What now?" King growled.

"Beats me," Thornhill said. "What are they so quiet about?"

"It's another trick," Barkley said cynically.

It was a trick. But it was showmanship too. Five large orange paper circles, each with a huge 41 in the center, began to glow under the Southwestern basket.

The brilliant circles grew brighter and brighter, and then, in company with a tremendous explosion, the lights flashed on and Southwestern's five starters, each carrying a ball, broke through the circles. The band broke into a strident march, and the crowd went mad.

Chip and his State teammates were wholly unprepared and could only stand and stare as Bordon, Ralk, Perkins, Lloyd, and Munn each dribbled hard for the basket, stopped, jumped up, arms extending high above the rim, and calmly dropped a ball cleanly through the hoop. Then the remaining members of the Southwestern squad joined in, and every player dropped the ball, drawing a tremendous cheer each time. That was the treatment's grand finale. In a few minutes the real business of the evening was underway.

Chip got a quick introduction to the Southwestern playing techniques. He lined up against Reggie Ralk, and the big player gave Chip a quick, hard handclasp. Then Ralk turned away without a word. But when the ball left the official's hand for the tip-off, he turned and nearly knocked Chip to the floor as he leaped high in the air for the ball. Chip recovered quickly and shot a quick glance at the official, but there was no whistle. *Well,* Chip thought, *so much for the principle of rough play being an issue for Southwestern.*

That first play set the pattern. Southwestern moved the ball until Bordon or Ralk got a good shot. Then Perkins joined in, and the three of them pounded the board, following the shot if it was unsuccessful and tapping the ball up and up and up again until it fell through the hoop.

The champions played a tight man-to-man defense, each player picking up his assigned opponent at the ten-second line and sticking to him like glue. When a State player tried to drive through, he always ran into an elbow. If he succeeded in getting ahead of his opponent, a clutching hand checked him. Although the officials called a few of the fouls, they were few and far between, and the result was more like a pickup game on the playground than collegiate basketball. It seemed the officials overlooked almost everything short of a knockdown.

But it was effective. And it stopped Corrigan's four-man weave before it could get started. State's attack degenerated into a mad scramble. It was every man for himself. The Southwestern players were openly contemptuous of State's efforts and kept up a derisive chatter. And if the purpose behind the display of poor sportsmanship was to upset their opponents, it was highly successful.

Chip was indignant and filled with bitterness. The treatment had been humiliating, but this was worse. He forgot all about blending in with the veterans and concentrated on trying to beat Southwestern all by himself. Never before had Chip forgotten the importance of team play; now he concentrated on putting the ball through the hoop at every opportunity. On the defense, he gave Ralk as good as he received. Several times he stole the ball away and dribbled the length of the court for a score.

The Southwestern fans were unfriendly, but they were, after all, rabid basketball fans. They had seldom seen an individual performance to match Chip's perfect play, and their applause, modest at first, gradually increased with each brilliant play. But Chip couldn't do it all, and despite his sixteen points, Southwestern led at the half: 39-29.

Corrigan was the last to reach the visitor's locker room, and the expression clouding his face clearly expressed his feelings. "This is disgraceful!" he raged. "In all my years as a player and as a coach, I have never seen anything like it.

"For two cents I'd tell you to dress and we'd pull out of here right now! But they'd like that! No, I won't put myself in their class. We'll fight it out! And we'll keep our heads and show them all—coach, team, fans, and everyone else—how this game is meant to be played. Sportsmanship? They don't know the meaning of the word!

"All right, I guess I haven't been much help. But there isn't much I can tell you to do against this kind of basketball . . . or officiating either! But we'll play clean if it kills us. That will hurt them more than a whipping."

Chip had never felt so eager to play. When the teams lined up for State's second-half throw-in, Chip played decoy and watched Ralk out of the corner of his eye. The official handed the ball to Gowdy at midcourt. Ralk tried to repeat his first trick as the ball flew toward Chip. But Chip beat him to it, took off a split second before the big all-American got started, and got the ball. Before Ralk regained his balance, Chip had started his dribble.

Ralk twisted around and followed Chip clear to the basket, trying to stop the shot, but Chip released the ball with his inside hand and Ralk hacked the wrong arm. This time the foul was right out in the open for everyone to see. Impossible to miss, impossible to overlook, and impossible not to call. The ball swished through the net just as the referee blasted his whistle.

Chip toed the free-throw line and dropped the ball cleanly through the basket; the three-point play made the score Southwestern 39, State 32.

Lloyd and Munn brought the ball upcourt and passed it to Ralk. He passed to Bordon on the pivot, but King blocked the big center's shot with a tremendous leap. Barkley drifted back, got the ball, and fired it to Chip on the sideline halfway up the court. Before Ralk could reach him, Chip dribbled downcourt, along the baseline, and around under the basket. He faked the hook shot, and when Ralk left his feet, Chip pivoted back and calmly banked the ball against the backboard and into the basket for two points.

"My, my," Barkley commented. "Did you see that? An all-American leaving his feet on the defense."

It was a beautiful play, and hostile as they were, the fans paid tribute with a spatter of applause. A few boos directed at the Southwestern team punctured the air.

Ralk was boiling. He grabbed the ball, stepped out of bounds, and passed to Munn. Or *tried* to pass! Chip timed it just right, pivoted toward Munn, and caught the ball. Taking one long step, Chip neatly dropped the ball through the hoop and took his defensive position. That made the score Southwestern 39, State 36. The fans were in a frenzy. Southwestern hadn't scored a point in the second half yet!

"THE TREATMENT"

Munn took the ball out of bounds this time, and Chip leeched onto Ralk, dogging him every step up the court. Bordon and Perkins tried to help Ralk, broke out behind Chip, and set up a double block. It worked! Ralk cut for the basket, and Chip was trapped. He couldn't get through or around Bordon and Perkins, so he took a chance and broke for the State basket.

Just as if it had been rehearsed, Bill King dropped back. And when Munn floated a soft pass over the heads of Bordon and Perkins toward Ralk for one of his patented slam dunks, Bill leaped high in the air, caught the ball in his huge hands, and winged it downcourt toward the State basket. Ralk saw King leap and turned and sprinted after Chip.

Chip had guessed right and was on top of the ball. He caught up to the ball on its first bounce and continued with a hard drive straight for the goal. He was out in front, all alone and in the clear. Behind him, Ralk was sprinting toward him. Chip took his last dribble and seemed to float toward the basket and through the air.

Just as he released the ball for the layup shot over the front rim, Ralk made a desperate leap over Chip's shoulder and tried to hit the ball. But he was too late; the momentum of his charge carried him into Chip's back. The charge sent Chip flying feetfirst into the padded support behind the basket. But the shot was perfect and cleared the rim. Chip saw it bob through the net, and then he heard the official's whistle blast for the foul.

Chip grinned and scrambled to his knees. Then he felt the pain. He got to his feet, made a step, and found that his right leg couldn't support his weight. He took another step toward the free-throw line and stopped. He couldn't walk!

CHAPTER 10

The Way It Was Meant to Be Played

MURPHY KELLY was off the bench and out on the floor before the official got the whistle out of his mouth. As Chip stood there, swaying on his one good leg, the turmoil of the crowd quieted just as it had before the game. Chip's teammates circled anxiously around him, ominously silent as Kelly examined the knee. "Don't try to stand on it, Chip," Kelly said sharply. "Speed, give me a hand."

Murph and Speed helped Chip to the sideline and through the aisle leading to the State locker room. Then, almost as if ashamed of their conduct, the crowd began to applaud. As the trio disappeared from view, the applause reached a voluminous thunder and continued, unabated, until play resumed on the floor.

Corrigan was furious. He followed Chip, whose arms were draped over Kelly and Speed, to the end of the floor, and as he walked back in front of the Southwestern bench, it was obvious he was restraining his temper with difficulty. He gave Jeff Habley a long, fierce look before continuing back to his own bench, where the State squad was grouped close together, glaring angrily at the Southwestern players.

"Skip it!" he ordered shortly. "Keep your heads. Remember, we're trying to give these people a lesson in sportsmanship.

"All right, Jimmy, you're in for Chip. You'll shoot the free throw."

Jimmy was trembling with ill-suppressed fury. His jaw was set in a grim line, and his dark eyes were flashing dangerously. Without a word he turned and dashed out on the floor.

"Jimmy!" Corrigan yelled. "Report!"

Jimmy turned back toward the scorers' table. The man with the official book acknowledged the intent and waved him into the game. The referee nodded and handed Jimmy the ball, and the little fighter walked to the free-throw line. He bounced the ball to gain time and then took the shot. The ball swished through the net to tie the score: Southwestern 39, State 39.

Southwestern's Bordon caught the ball as it cleared the net, and he stepped quickly out of bounds. Then he passed to Lloyd in the corner, and the fleet guard dribbled quickly upcourt. Jimmy picked Ralk up at the ten-second line and stuck with him like gum on a shoe. The big guard contemptuously ignored Jimmy, relaxed, and then suddenly cut for the basket, trying to pick Jimmy off on the high post that Bordon had set up on the free-throw line. But Jimmy was too fast. He darted between Ralk and Bordon, covering Ralk like a blanket.

Bill King, at six-nine, was two inches shorter than Bordon. But he had the weight to match the big all-American star's mad rushes, and he was giving Two-Ton as good as he received. King saw the play coming and dropped back to make the switch. But when he saw Jimmy wouldn't need help, he grinned appreciatively. "Nice going, Jimmy!" he called. "Stay! Stay!"

"Atta baby, Jimmy," Barkley called encouragingly. "Stick with him!"

Ralk didn't like the taunt in Barkley's voice and tried one of his tricks. He slowed down, yawned, and glanced at a spectator on the sideline. Then Reggie suddenly accelerated and tried to outrace Jimmy to the basket. The change-of-pace trick was good but not fast enough, and Ralk was surprised to find Jimmy right in his path.

Ralk could have stopped or changed direction, but he didn't even try; he mouthed something angrily and crashed into and over the little guard, knocking Jimmy to the floor. It was a deliberate charging foul and obvious to everyone.

The referee blasted his whistle and stooped to help Jimmy to his feet. "You all right?" he asked solicitously.

Barkley lost his head and charged toward Ralk. "That's dirty!" he cried. "What are you trying to do?"

Both benches had emptied, and players from both teams were edging out on to the floor. The referee blasted his whistle again and dashed between Barkley and Ralk. "Knock it off, you two," he threatened, "or out you go, both of you!" He turned toward the benches flanking the scorers' table. "You sit down too!" he stormed. "All of you!"

The official moved in front of the scorers' table, extending his arms above his head, crossed at the wrists to indicate an intentional foul. His fingers then flashed the player charged with the foul. "Foul is on number 42 in white. State's shooting two free throws for the intentional foul. After the free throws, State gets the ball out of bounds."

Meanwhile, Jimmy had reached the free-throw line, walking unsteadily but attempting to conceal the effect of the collision. But he was far from all right, and he took all the time he could, bouncing the ball until the official warned him. The first shot bounced off the metal ring. Jimmy readied for his second shot. This time, the ball whizzed straight and true. State was out in front of the national champions by a single point, with twelve minutes left to play!

Southwestern's captain, Reggie Ralk, called time, and his teammates looked in disbelief at the scoreboard. The score: State 40, Southwestern 39.

In the State locker room, Chip was lying on the trainers' table, and the Southwestern doctor was examining his leg when Corrigan stuck his head in the door. "How is it, Murph?" he asked.

The doctor answered. "He's a lucky young man. The knee is a little swollen, and he'll probably be pretty stiff for a few days."

"What about the rest of the game?" Chip queried.

"No way, son. But we'll have you up before the game is over."

"What's the score, Coach?" Chip asked.

Corrigan grinned. "We're ahead. Jimmy sank your free throw and just threw in another on an intentional foul; Southwestern called time. Your teammates are worried. They'll be glad to know you're all right."

"Not all right, Coach," the doctor said. "Far from it. But at least there's nothing major. I'd advise you to get him to your team doctor as soon as you get home."

"Murph will take care of that," Corrigan said. "Thanks a lot, Doc. Well, I've got to get back and hold that lead."

After Corrigan left, the doctor wrapped Chip's knee. "Well, I guess I can't do anything more for you. Sorry you got hurt. I'd like to have seen some more of you in action. How come you got away from Jeff Habley? I thought he knew every star in the country."

"My dad went to State," Chip said simply. "Besides, all my friends go there, and it's our state university. We're pretty proud of our school."

When the door closed, Kelly turned back to Chip. "Now you stay put, Chip, and I'll get back to the bench. Might be a good thing to get dressed before the game is over. I'll send in one of the managers to help you and update the score for you."

Chip was on the table when the manager appeared. The manager's face told the story. "No good! Got us down by five, 46 to 41. Knee feel better? Good. I'll be back."

Chip was dressed the next time the manager returned. "Man," he said in disgust. "I've seen a lot of basketball, but I've never seen any team play as dirty as that bunch. I don't know how they get away with it."

"What's the score now?"

The manager shook his head glumly. "Hate to tell you. Nineteen points down, 66-47. About five minutes left to play. Guess I'd better go back."

Chip packed his gear and sat back down on the table. He could hear the roar of the crowd, and then he heard the buzzer ending the game. Seconds later, the door opened and his teammates straggled in, thoroughly beaten and discouraged and thoroughly aroused with anger. They were in no mood to talk about the game, but despite their anger and dejection, they didn't forget Chip.

And the brief smiles of relief that crossed their lips when they learned the extent of his injury moved deep into Chip's heart.

Yes, he sure was proud of his school and his teammates and his team—fighting all the way and losing like sportsmen, playing the game as it was meant to be played, hard and all out, but clean and by the rules.

The silent players dressed quickly, and the bus that whisked them away from the Southwestern University Arena couldn't do it fast enough. The players filed dejectedly into their hotel team room at Southwestern Inn for last words from Coach Corrigan. The meeting was short, and the players happily sought refuge back in their rooms.

Jimmy, Speed, Sky Bollinger, and Chip had adjoining rooms. Chip skillfully led the conversation around to the game.

"We were terrible," Sky said. "If I ever play bad basketball like that again, I'll turn in my uniform. If it hadn't been for Jimmy, we wouldn't have scored fifty points."

"I never played football," Jimmy said grimly, "but if it's any worse than that kind of basketball . . . ."

"You took care of Ralk, all right," Speed said. "Tied him in knots."

"I wish someone would explain to me how Southwestern can get away with that kind of basketball," Jimmy said. "They surely can't play that way when they're on the road and in the tournaments."

"Rock scouted them when they were away from home," Speed said shortly. "You know what he told us."

"It's probably not right, but when they ran through that orange paper and drove for the basket, I was really hoping they'd throw down some dunks in the warm-up to get technicals."

Speed laughed. "Sky, they're too smart for that. They know the rules."

"I guess it's a different league," Sky said thoughtfully. "They're big time, and we're just another team."

"That's not it," Jimmy objected. "The rules are supposed to be the same for every team in every game. They play as if they wrote the rules."

"Anyone can beat the rules," Chip said softly. "Anyone who wants to play that kind of basketball."

"But how about the officials?" Jimmy persisted. "How come they let them get away with charging and pushing and tripping and busting you in the nose with their elbows and things like that?"

"Because they're Southwestern," Speed said. "They're the national champs. They can get away with murder."

"Not quite," Chip protested. "They just happen to be clever. It will catch up with them."

Speed smiled ruefully. "Then it better hurry up. Most of them are seniors, and they'll be out of school."

"I wish *we* could catch up with them," Jimmy said. "I'd like another chance on a different floor with that dirty bunch." He tried to draw a deep breath. "You know something? I never told Murph, but I think I've got a cracked rib."

"Tell him now," Chip urged.

Jimmy shook his head and smiled. "I'll tell him in the morning. He's had a rough night."

"I'll say he has," Sky agreed. "He works all the time and gives us grief and treats us like toddlers, but he'd give us his right arm. And way down underneath, he thinks anyone who plays for State is at the top of the world."

Speed nodded. "Right! Well, Sky, let's hit the rack. You take the bed next to the phone."

"Why me?"

"So your long arms can reach out and grab the phone for Murph's wake-up call before it bothers me. Everybody knows the best sleep is that five minutes of rest after the clock goes off."

With the lights out and ESPN flashing college basketball scores across the screen, Jimmy continued the conversation. He was still disturbed by the humiliation and the dirty play. "It isn't fair," he said. "Remember when we were talking that Sunday? About sportsmanship and your Golden Rule?"

"We'll have another chance, Jimmy. In the tournament, maybe."

"I'd give anything in the world to get even with that bunch."

Chip nodded. "I know. I feel the same way. They're fine players and don't have to play dirty to win. That's what I can't understand."

"Do you really think we'll have a chance in the tournament?"

"Every team has a chance. It would be nice to win it in your own hometown, with your family there to see you do it."

"Pop wouldn't walk across the street to see the president of the United States box the queen of England."

"You mean he doesn't like sports?"

"That's right. In fact, he doesn't even know I'm playing. He'd hit the ceiling if he knew I wasn't spending every waking moment studying. You know the old saying: 'Sleep five hours and fail. Sleep four hours and pass.'"

"Won't he find out when we play Wilson University?"

"I don't think so."

"But how about the papers?"

"He never reads American papers, especially the sports pages. You won't believe it, but we don't even have a phone in the restaurant."

"No phone? Why not?"

"Pop thinks it would mean we were showing our prosperity."

"Really? Guess I always thought of it just as a tool for business—like everybody having computers at State—it's part of everyday life. What's wrong with a phone in the restaurant?"

"Nothing as far as I'm concerned, but that's the way Pop is. He sees it as being extravagant and wasteful since we have a phone at home."

"You're kidding."

"I was never more serious. You ought to see our restaurant. It's dark and decorated in red—that's a favorite Chinese color—with these grotesque paintings of flowers and birds all over the place. And if a stray dog or cat wanders in, it becomes a member of the family just like that because it's a sign of good luck. My sisters find homes for them, or there wouldn't be anything in the place but cats."

"Now you *are* kidding."

"No, I'm not. On my word of honor."

"Maybe you can change all that when you get through college," Chip suggested, yawning.

Jimmy shrugged. "*If* I get through college," he repeated. "The way things are going at home, I'll be lucky to get through this semester."

"Business can't be that bad."

"Well," Jimmy admitted, "it might not be so bad if Pop could keep his help happy. But they're always leaving for better pay or better hours. I guess that's one of the biggest troubles with the restaurant. If he'd only listen to

Tommy and me. We want to keep the place Chinese, but if we could brighten it up and serve more items on the menu—with English translations—everything would be great. We've got a great location."

Jimmy stopped suddenly and shook his head. "There I go again, bothering you with my family troubles."

"A friend's troubles are never a bother, Jimmy."

CHAPTER 11

Subtle as a Technical Foul

LI HONG "JIMMY" CHUNG and Chip shared the sports headlines in the University papers the next day. The *News* said that Hilton had been the best player on the floor until he was injured and that Jimmy Chung deserved those honors for the rest of the game. The *Herald* played up the fact that State held the lead early in the second half and printed pictures of Chip and Jimmy.

The campus chatter was not so much about State's defeat as Southwestern's forty-first consecutive victory and the almost unbelievable home-floor consecutive winning streak of 141 games.

Some mentioned the extremely rough and reckless play and the poor officiating, but the students couldn't get the players to talk much about that part of the game. Coaches Corrigan and Rockwell and their players didn't believe in excuses.

Chip's knee had stiffened up during the flight from

SUBTLE AS A TECHNICAL FOUL

Hawthorn to University, and he walked several extra blocks on his way to report to Murph Kelly. Kelly was expecting him. "You walk pretty good," Kelly said in his usual gruff manner. "Any pain?"

"None at all, Murph. Just feels tight and tired."

"Well, come on. Might as well get the bad news. I gave Doc the X rays first thing this morning. He said to bring you right up."

There was no waiting, and the physician's assistant, Sondra Ruiz, ushered Chip and Kelly directly into one of the examining rooms. Dr. Mike Terring smiled a greeting and motioned Chip toward the table. "Let's have a look-see. Couldn't find anything wrong with it in the X rays. Hmmm. Not too bad. Hurt when you walk?"

"No, sir."

"Murph's good work at the game helped. Yes, it's secure enough. Let him exercise lightly, Murph, but watch him."

"Want him to dress?"

"Not today. Perhaps Saturday."

"We've got a game on Saturday," Chip suggested.

Terring smiled. "We'll see."

At practice, Chip sat up in the bleachers and watched. Corrigan was experimenting with a new lineup that included Barkley, King, Di Santis, Thornhill, and Chung. But, just as before, Jimmy couldn't blend into the set attack.

"He's a natural floor leader for a more wide-open game," Chip breathed. "I wish Coach would give Speed, Sky, Bitsy, Jimmy, and me a chance to use the fast break and a little more of a free attack."

Chip left early and walked slowly toward Main Street, trying to keep from limping. When he reached

Main and Tenth, he continued on down to Pete's Place for something to eat before going to work. Pete was getting ready for the dinner rush and talked to Chip while he worked.

"Jimmy's the best cook and waiter I ever had!"

"Is that so?" a cheery voice demanded. Jimmy entered just in time to hear Pete's words. "Well, I should be! Pop always had trouble with his cooks, and I had to fill in. Want me to eat now, Pete?"

Pete nodded. "Sure, kiddo. Sit down there with Chip."

While Jimmy was eating Pete's roast beef special, he continued. "Cooks are very special in China, Chip."

"I guess that's true all over the world. Especially the chefs."

"You couldn't tell Pop that. Labor means nothing to him. To Pop, everything has a material value. So he brings in a lot of cheap, inexperienced labor, and trains them very well. Pretty soon they learn the kind of wages cooks and waiters get at other places and they quit. Pop just can't seem to understand that the human element enters into everything, even cooking and waiting tables. So he's really training workers for other restaurants."

"Seems everyone wants to make more money."

"You know, money isn't everything, Chip. The Chinese of Pop's generation were different in that respect. Peace, comfort, and security were more important to them than actual wages. But Pop doesn't understand that wages have more importance today."

"Speaking of wages, I better go earn mine. See you after work."

Chip had a visitor at about nine o'clock. Henry Rockwell sauntered into the stockroom, and Chip greeted him warmly. There was a strong bond between Chip and the veteran mentor, and whenever Chip experienced some sort of difficulty, Rockwell invariably turned up.

"Just got back from the scouting trip and thought I'd check up on this knee business myself," Rockwell said. "Is it all right or not?"

"It's stiff and sore, but there's no real pain, Coach. And I can use it fine, or at least pretty well."

"I checked with Doc Terring, and he said the same thing, but I wanted to make sure. Do you think Ralk fouled you deliberately?"

"I don't know, Coach. I didn't see him. I took the shot, and he must have dived over my shoulder to stop it. All I know is that he knocked me for a loop."

"What do you think of Southwestern's style of play?"

"I think the same as you," Chip replied wryly.

Rockwell shrugged. "By the way, what would you think of our chances in another game with them? With good officiating and everyone—including yourself, naturally—in good shape?"

"I don't know, Coach. They're good! They stopped our set attack cold."

"How about *our* defense?"

"They didn't have much trouble scoring on us. We're not big enough to stop them under the boards."

Rockwell nodded thoughtfully and paced back and forth across the room. "You're right, Chip. You can't play the other fellow's game and expect to win."

"I think the press attack you taught us in Valley Falls would give them a lot of trouble."

"Why?"

"They don't like to run, or they don't appear to like it. Maybe it's because they haven't had to run. They use a strong collapsing defense and a deliberate power attack with a strong follow-in. I was thinking that if a team played them all over the court man-to-man and switched on every cross and took a lot of chances, they might get upset."

"But we don't have that kind of a team, Chip."

"Not the first five, no. But Jimmy Chung would be terrific in an all-court press, and Speed, Bitsy, and Sky are fast and can run all night."

"And if Chip Hilton's knee were in good shape," Rockwell added, smiling, "you think it would be a pretty fair pressing team. Right? So do I! The tough part is that you're all sophomores, except Jimmy. And Coach Corrigan is dead set on his weave. But it's something to think about. I'm glad you're all right, but I want you to promise me you will stop the second your knee acts up. OK? Guess I'll be running along. See you tomorrow."

Early the next afternoon, Jim Corrigan and Henry Rockwell happened along while Kelly was fastening a brace on Chip's knee.

"He's coming along fine, Coach," Kelly said. "Gonna let him work out this afternoon or at least do a little shooting."

"I'm glad to hear that," Corrigan said. "How about the game tomorrow night?"

"He's coming in tomorrow morning and again in the afternoon, and Doc said he'd know by that time. He said he'd be ready for the Wilson game."

Corrigan and Rockwell walked slowly up the steps to the office. Settling themselves comfortably in their chairs, they talked about Chip and the team in general. Corrigan was depressed, and Rockwell tried to cheer him up.

"One and three," Corrigan said gloomily. "What a record! What's wrong with the team, Rock?"

SUBTLE AS A TECHNICAL FOUL

"It's a pretty tough schedule."

"Tough for other teams too. I thought we were going to have a great year. We certainly have plenty of talent."

"It's early," Rockwell said cheerfully. "Did you ever think about using two teams? One year I had a bunch of veterans and some youngsters almost as wild as the Southwestern fans. They were a whole lot like Reardon, Morris, Chung, and Bollinger.

"I used them as a sort of change-of-pace outfit; I played the veterans for part of the game and then stuck in the kids. It was something to see. Fans loved it. It might be the answer to your problem."

Corrigan frowned thoughtfully and studied the veteran coach with knowing eyes. "I suppose you would play Hilton with that bunch."

Rockwell nodded gravely. "Oh, sure."

"Oh, sure!" Corrigan mimicked. "You know something, Rock," he continued thoughtfully, "you're about as subtle as a technical foul." He banged his fist down on the desk. "All right, I'll give it a try. Tomorrow night!"

Dr. Terring and Murph Kelly were waiting when Chip reported at nine o'clock Saturday morning. After the brace was removed, Dr. Terring checked the knee carefully. Then he replaced the brace, went up on the gym floor, and had Chip run around the court several times. Then Terring checked the knee carefully again. "All right, Murph," he said at last, "let's see him back here this afternoon."

"What about the game?"

"I'll talk to you about that later."

Following Terring's exam that afternoon, Chip felt so good he wanted to sprint all the way to Grayson's; he was convinced he would be ready to play that night. But Murph Kelly and Coach Corrigan had other ideas.

In the locker room, Kelly checked the brace and told him he could dress. Chip suited up and waited hopefully during Corrigan's pregame talk.

"This one is a must! So we're going to try something new. We're going to match man-to-man when we line up, but when they cross on the offense, we're going to switch. And we'll take a few chances and try to make some interceptions.

"On the offense, we'll fast-break when we get the chance, and if we can't get a three-on-two or a two-on-one situation, we'll go into the weave. All right. We'll start with Barkley, Thornhill, King, Di Santis, and Chung."

In the pregame warm-up drill, Chip loosened up gradually, favoring his good leg but moving without pain. But he wasn't ready and he knew it. And so did Murph Kelly and Coach Corrigan. They were watching him closely.

"What do you think, Murph? What did Doc Terring say?"

"He said to use him if you had to, but only for a few minutes at a time. Better let him sit for awhile."

"Hope I don't need him. But we've got to win this one, or we're in a deep hole."

So Chip rode the bench and suffered with the fans as the Vikings of Northern State University slowly but surely drew away from the desperate Statesmen. Jimmy was magnificent on the defense, stealing the ball and dribbling the length of the court for several quick scores. And when State managed to work a fast break, he was the spearhead of the attack. But he was blunted when State went into the weave; his lightning ability to take advantage of openings was too fast for the veterans, and time after time they failed to hit him with the ball.

With the score 40 to 25 in favor of the visitors and

five minutes left to play in the first half, Corrigan put Chip in for Di Santis. State took on new life right away. Chip hit with three jumpers and a free throw, and the teams left the court with the scoreboard reading Northern State 41, State 32.

State looked better in the second half. Corrigan used the same lineup that started the game, and the teams battled on even terms. But even terms couldn't make up the deficit, and with just over fourteen minutes left in the game, Northern State led 55-44.

When the players gathered in front of the bench, Corrigan almost shocked them out of their uniforms. "All right," he said decisively, "we're going to use the press. I want you to forget all about the weave and the slow advance and chase them all over the court. Let's go!"

Chip and the other bench warmers who had surrounded the starters dropped back down on the bench. Chip nudged Speed and glanced significantly at Bitsy Reardon. Bitsy nodded. This was the kind of basketball they liked.

Out on the floor, the veterans were attempting the press. But it backfired. They had been drilled too long in Corrigan's deliberate advance and programmed weave; they switched at the wrong time, failed to cover up on a try for an interception, and, with the exception of Jimmy, completely botched up the game. Northern State gleefully took advantage of State's misplays, and when Corrigan yelled for time, the visitors led 68-51, with eight minutes left to play.

"All right, Hilton! Reardon! Bollinger! Morris! Report for Barkley, Thornhill, Di Santis, and King. Chung stays in!"

Chip and his sophomore pals raced to the scoring table and back to surround Corrigan and Chung. "Now listen!" Corrigan rasped excitedly. "Same thing! Press 'em all over the court. Take chances! Eight minutes and seventeen points behind. Nothing to lose! Go get 'em!"

They got 'em!

With lightning-fast reflexes, Speed, Jimmy, and Bitsy were superior judges of distance and timing. They were hot after interceptions and swarmed all over Northern State's small men. Sky and Chip paired up against the two big men and froze them clear out of the play.

The State fans could scarcely follow the lightning-fast action on the floor, but they could see the scoreboard, and as the numbers under the home-team position flickered again and again, they realized something tremendous was happening to their team. And they wanted to be a part of it. They rose to their feet en masse and yelled and screamed and stamped until it seemed that the building would come tumbling down.

"Go, State! C'mon, Chung!"

The student body started to chant, "Chung! Chung! Chung! Chung!"

Jimmy was all over the floor, making interceptions, double-teaming opponents, dribbling furiously for the State goal, and drawing two and sometimes three of the opponents to him in a vain attempt to stop his mad progress toward the basket. Then Jimmy would slip the ball to Speed or Bitsy for an easy layup or, more often, fire the ball back to Chip for an open three-point shot.

Their on-court chatter told Chip to remain in the backcourt and take no chances with his knee. He waited for Jimmy, Speed, or Bitsy to get the ball. Sky was back with him and did most of the running, covering up so that Chip could protect his knee.

SUBTLE AS A TECHNICAL FOUL

Chip took his jump shots when none of his team-mates were open, and without bearing down on his knee, he got twelve of the twenty-six points State scored in those mad eight minutes. Northern State battled furiously but couldn't hold the lead. Chip tied the score at 75-75 with thirty seconds left to play. Jimmy wrapped it up with an interception and a two-pointer a split second before the buzzer.

The game ended with the fans, the veterans on the bench, the coaches, and the visiting players completely exhausted. The final score: State 77, Northern State University 75.

CHAPTER 12

The Team's the Thing

STATE'S COCAPTAINS were the first to reach Jimmy after the final buzzer. Kirk and Andy ushered him off the court, patting him on the back and ruffling his hair all the way to the locker room. The fans gave Jimmy a standing ovation until he passed from sight. Jimmy had arrived at the door of stardom! He had thrilled every State supporter with his dazzling performance in the action-packed, last-minute victory surge. He had won almost single-handedly a game most fans had given up as lost.

Chip, Speed, Bitsy, and Sky came in for their share of the glory when the team reached the locker room, and upstairs in the basketball office, Jim Corrigan dropped wearily down in his chair and breathed a deep sigh of relief.

Rockwell settled himself comfortably in his favorite chair and grinned appreciatively at the happy coach. "That was one for the books," he said. "Nice comeback."

"Thanks to your idea," Corrigan said thankfully. "It was your idea and it worked. I've been using the kids all wrong. They put on the press as if they had played that way all their lives. Jimmy Chung was sensational."

"Chip wasn't bad," Rockwell added dryly. "By the way, he suggested the press and the sophomore combination with Chung to me the other day. I just passed it on to you. I'm glad I did."

"Chip's not only a great player; he also uses his head," Corrigan replied. "And what an eye! I never saw anyone shoot like he can. What a combination he and Jimmy make."

"You had me wondering a bit when you put on the press with Barkley and Thornhill and the other starters."

"I had to do that, Rock. Had to give the veterans a chance at it so they would find out they couldn't handle it. It worked out all right, but it was too close for comfort."

"Going to stick with it?"

"Sure! I'm going to use your suggestion. I think it gives us another dimension. But I think it will be good strategy to keep the press team under wraps and use it only when conditions merit. Sound OK to you?"

"It sure does. In fact, that's the way I've always used the press. I had a special team that could handle it and worked them on every phase of it every day. Then, when I wanted to surprise a team or when we couldn't match up with our regular style, I'd send in the press team."

Corrigan shot forward in his chair. "Say," he said excitedly, "that gives me an idea! We won't get far playing straight against the tough teams in the tournament. We haven't got the horses. But if we worked the kids on the press every day, we might even surprise Southwestern.

"Man, that's one team every coach in the country would like to see lose. Especially me! I'll never get over the treatment they gave us last week. You think the press would work against them?"

"It's worth trying. Chip thinks it will work." Rockwell hesitated and stroked his chin reflectively. "Er—as a suggestion, Jim, why don't you concentrate on the kids and try to get along without the press until the tournament? I believe you can beat Wilson University and Cathedral without the press. Then, if you can get by in the tournament without using it until you run into Southwestern—if you run into them—maybe you can engineer the greatest upset of all times."

"It would be just our luck to draw them in the first round."

"All the better," Rockwell said crisply. "Then you *would* surprise them. Well, I guess I'll go home." He paused at the door. "Tonight you can sleep, right? Stop worrying, Jim. You've got a good team."

Chip and Jimmy managed to get away from their happy teammates and started for work. Chip was tired and tempted to go home, but Grayson's was exceptionally busy on game nights. So he trudged along with Jimmy, thankful that the training curfew was not in effect. Then they got a break. A car screeched to a stop beside them, and the door swung open. "Want a ride, guys? We're going right past Grayson's."

Chip peered in at the speaker and recognized Sky Bollinger's father. "Got room for both of us?"

Mr. Bollinger smiled. "Absolutely. Plenty of room. Wanted to talk to you anyway. Some game you guys put up tonight. Move over, Bobby. Chip, you know Mrs. Bollinger and Bobby, I guess."

THE TEAM'S THE THING

He extended his hand toward the backseat to Jimmy. "My name is Mr. Bollinger. I'm Sky's father. This is Mrs. Bollinger. Shake hands with Bobby. Sure glad to meet you, Jimmy. I never saw anyone put on a passing exhibition in my life like you put on tonight. Some shooting, Chip. Sky's coming along, right, Chip? Thanks to you."

He looked into the rearview mirror and caught Jimmy's eyes. "Guess you didn't know Chip here helped me straighten out my whole family last year, did you?"

"Now, now," Mrs. Bollinger protested.

"Well, it's true, isn't it? He made Bobby here shooting champion of the country in his class and a man of Sky, straightened him out until he's a pretty fair ballplayer now. I hope Corrigan keeps you guys together as a team. Played myself a few years back, and I know a real team when I see it."

Trudy Bollinger laughed. "A few years . . . ."

Chip and Jimmy listened to Mr. Bollinger all the way to Grayson's. When they got out of the car, they accepted an invitation to dinner at the Bollingers' the next afternoon.

"Wow!" Jimmy said. "No wonder Sky can run. He'd have to be fast to escape that verbal barrage."

"He's a nice man," Chip said, laughing, "but he's hoop crazy. We'll have a good time at their house. They're real nice people. See you after work."

Jimmy impulsively grasped Chip by the arm. "Take care of that leg, Chip," he said. "We haven't got much of a team without you." He hesitated a moment. "Another thing. I couldn't help hearing all the nice things Mr. Bollinger was saying, and I just want you to know he expressed my sentiments, too, except that he's better qualified to put them into words. I guess you know what I mean. See you later."

TOURNAMENT CRISIS

Soapy Smith, Fireball Finley, and Philip Whittemore were struggling to keep up with the fountain demands of their noisy customers, but they spotted Chip as soon as he came through the door. "Hey, Chip! Big win!"

The greeting was taken up by the customers, and Chip had a difficult time getting through the crowd. He breathed a sigh of relief when he reached the stockroom, but he caught it again from his assistant, Isaiah. While Isaiah was peppering him with questions about the game, Chip hustled into an extra polo shirt and white slacks. His job was in the stockroom, but he always helped his friends at the fountain when there was a big rush.

Meanwhile, business was booming at Pete's Place. This after-game rush was all new to Pete. A few of the college students who appreciated good food at inexpensive prices had always favored Pete's Place, but with the addition of Jimmy to the staff, the campus business had increased by leaps and bounds.

Tonight, Pete couldn't keep up with the rush. But he loved it! The customers all wanted to talk about the game, and Jimmy was the center of attention. But Jimmy didn't stop his work to talk; he worked as he played basketball, his hands and his feet flying, yet he was doing the work of three waiters. Pete kept going, too, but he listened avidly to the conversations.

"Nice going, Jimmy! What's the coach been saving you for?"

"You and Hilton got a partnership? He takes the shots and all you gotta do is get the ball. Some system."

Jimmy grinned happily. "If you could shoot like Hilton, I'd get the ball for you too!"

The regular customers who sat on the stools in front of the counter had listened to the student chatter. Now one of them ventured into the conversation. "Your team won't last long in that tournament up in Springfield. That's my hometown, and I've seen some of the teams that go to the invitational; they get the best."

"Springfield's my hometown too," Jimmy replied. "I've seen a lot of those tournaments. We're going to win this one."

"You guys better take Wilson and Cathedral first," one of the students bantered.

"We'll take 'em!" Jimmy said. "We'll take 'em all if Chip's knee holds up."

"He didn't move very much tonight."

"You have to move on that big court in Wilson's new gym," the man who had spoken previously observed. "It's more like a football field than a basketball court."

"We can move."

"How about Hilton? How about his knee?"

Jimmy was ready for that question. "He'll run when the time comes," he said confidently.

"That's the court they use for the tournament, isn't it?"

"Sure is! Wilson's in the tournament too."

"Seems to me they get all the breaks. People who know tell me a home court means a ten- to fifteen-point advantage for the home team."

"The team is the thing!" Jimmy countered. "Not the court!"

"Wilson *is* one of the best in the country," another regular chimed in.

"Yes, and they'll be laying for you, Jimmy. They'll be out to show up the hometown boy."

Jimmy nodded grimly. "I know. I've been waiting for a chance at them too. Ever since I was in high school."

Later, when Chip and Soapy came in for a snack before going home, Pete's Place was still filled. Pete and Jimmy were working side by side behind the counter, keeping up a constant chatter with the hungry customers. Pete's face was covered with perspiration, but Jimmy looked cool and composed.

"Either of you gentlemen lookin' for a job?" Pete asked, mopping his forehead and winking at Jimmy. "Business is so good, Jimmy and I are thinkin' about goin' to Florida for the rest of the winter."

"How about selling the place?" Soapy laughed. "I've got a couple of old dollars I'm not using. But I'd have to get the food inventory."

"Talk to my partner," Pete said, jerking a thumb in Jimmy's direction. "It's up to him. Suppose you go along with these two gentlemen, Jimmy, and discuss the terms."

It was good fun, but while the three friends were walking home, the talk swung to basketball and struck a serious note.

"Southwestern won again," Jimmy said abruptly. "Number forty-two. I heard it on Gray's program. That's 142 in a row at home."

"No one seems to be able to stop them," Chip said.

"You'll stop 'em!" Soapy said stoutly. "In the tournament! Wait and see if I'm not right."

They continued, thinking about Southwestern and the tournament. When they reached the corner where Jimmy turned to go home, they stopped for a second. "The two big ambitions in my life right now," Jimmy said, "are first to beat Wilson on Wednesday night in Springfield and then to whip Southwestern in the tournament."

"Then you two better get some sleep," Soapy said.

"Going to church with us in the morning, Jimmy?"

"I'd like to, Chip."

"OK, we'll meet you right here at ten o'clock."

After church services the next morning, Soapy left for Mitzi Savrill's house, and Chip and Jimmy walked to the Bollingers. As Chip had promised, Jimmy had a wonderful time. Mr. Bollinger seemed content to listen to the basketball talk and plans for the tournament. Mrs. Bollinger was the star of the show. Dinner drew enthusiastic comments from the two guests and her family.

Bobby laughed. "Soapy doesn't know what he missed, does he, Chip?"

Chip was filling his plate again. "Soapy does have a reputation—and it's well deserved—when it comes to food."

"Mrs. Bollinger, this is the kind of food Pop ought to serve," Jimmy said. "I'm glad we don't have a game tonight. I don't think I can walk home."

Jimmy was still lauding Mrs. Bollinger's cooking when Chip left him later that afternoon. "My," Jimmy said, grinning and patting his stomach happily, "that beats Pete's Place by a mile. See you tomorrow morning in the library."

But Chip didn't see Jimmy the next morning. Jimmy wasn't at the library or with the crew at the student union. So Chip walked briskly across the campus and down Main Street. He passed Grayson's and turned down Tenth to Pete's Place. Pete was leaning on the cash register, staring moodily out the window.

"Have you seen Jimmy?" Chip asked.

Pete nodded slowly. "Yeah, I saw him," he said glumly. "Came in here first thing this morning looking like he'd lost his best friend. Said he had to quit, had to go home."

"Quit? You mean he quit the job?"

"That's right. He asked for his pay, and I gave it to him."

"But what about school?"

"Quit school too! Said he was shippin' his stuff home and for me to tell everybody good-bye. It's got me down. I don't care whether I keep this place open or not. . . . I couldn't have thought more of Jimmy if he was my own son."

CHAPTER 13

The Tea House

THE AMTRAK TRAIN travel time between University and Springfield was listed at slightly over six hours. But it seemed like sixty hours to Jimmy Chung. Ordinarily, he would have enjoyed the ride, read a little, sauntered forward to the dining car for a leisurely lunch, and probably entered into casual conversation with a fellow traveler. But not this trip. No airline could get him there before the next day, and the Greyhound bus wouldn't leave until late the next night . . . so Amtrak it was.

Jimmy sat alone in a seat by the window, gazing with sad, uninterested eyes at fields and farmhouses and small towns and roads and fences and trees and the never-ending line of telephone poles that whizzed past in a steady blur. He tried to tell himself that the phone call was a figment of his imagination, that the words his mother had spoken were wrong, that his father wasn't really seriously ill, that he didn't have to leave school.

Maybe it was all part of a bad dream. Maybe there wasn't any phone call, and maybe he wasn't even on this train.

But it was no use. He remembered how he had envisioned traveling to Springfield with the team to play against Wilson University. Suddenly the lump in his chest and his throat swelled up, and he felt that he couldn't bear the pain.

And just about then, back in University, Chip was standing beside the cashier reading the letter Jimmy had written and left for him at Grayson's.

> Sunday night
> Dear Chip,
>
> By the time you're reading this letter, I'll be almost home. My father is sick and it is necessary for me to go home and take care of the restaurant. I guess a lot of Pop's sickness is due to money matters and worry over the restaurant, and my place is with him and the family.
>
> Will you please explain to Coach Corrigan why I had to leave and say good-bye to the team and Coach Rockwell. I guess I will have to forget about college and basketball, but I'll never forget all the things you did for me.
> Always your friend,
> Jimmy

Chip didn't feel much like going to practice that afternoon. But he had to give Jimmy's message to Coach Corrigan, so he got an early start and walked slowly back to the campus and up to the basketball office. Coach Corrigan and Henry Rockwell were bending over some papers on the desk.

Corrigan looked up and motioned for Chip to come in. "Hiya, Chip," he said cheerfully. "You're early! Come on in. We're just looking over the Wilson scouting notes. Anything on your mind?"

"Quite a lot," Chip said quietly. "I'm afraid I've got some bad news." He handed Jimmy's letter to Coach Corrigan. "Jimmy has had to leave school."

"Leave school?" Corrigan echoed. "Oh, no!" He dropped down in his chair and read the letter without speaking. When he finished, he handed the letter to Rockwell. "What next?" he said bitterly.

Rockwell finished the letter and returned it to Chip. "Can't we get him back? Can't his father hire someone to run the place? Hasn't he got any brothers?"

"He has one brother, Coach, but he doesn't live at home."

"Can't they send for him? Wouldn't that make more sense than pulling Jimmy out of school and ruining a fine science career? I don't get it. I think we ought to call his father, Jim."

"Do you know Jimmy's telephone number in Springfield, Chip?" Corrigan asked.

"No, we never talked about it, Coach."

"How about the restaurant?"

Chip tried to explain about the phone and the eldest son and the rest of Jimmy's family difficulties, but Corrigan and Rockwell didn't understand. They sat there looking at each other, then at Chip, and back again, everything in their grim faces expressing disappointment.

"Well," Corrigan said at last, "we'll leave it in your hands. Just as soon as we get to Springfield, you check up with Jimmy and let us know what we can do to help. His future is in science, not the restaurant business. He needs to get back in school as soon as he can. I'll have our secretary call his professors to let them know the situation. Tell him we're counting on him playing against Wilson too."

"Jimmy is vital to our plans right now, Chip," Rockwell added. "In fact, he's the key to our whole tournament campaign, present company excepted."

News of Jimmy's difficulties quickly spread through the squad, and Corrigan might as well have called off practice as the scrimmage benefited none of the players. Jimmy's popularity had soared after his fine play against Northern State, and his loss was a blow to everyone.

After practice, a dejected Chip went to work. It was a long evening. Murph Kelly let Chip take part in a few of the drills the next afternoon and then checked out his knee. And that night when Chip dropped in to see Pete on his way home, his knee felt as good as new. Pete handed him a letter.

"Give this to Jimmy, Chip. And try to get him back, will you? If it's a matter of money, I can help. We don't have much, but he can have it."

"I think it's more a matter of family problems than money, Pete. Anyway, I'll know the whole story when I get back here Thursday."

Chip was asleep when Soapy came in from work, and the redhead didn't even turn on the light. And in the morning, Soapy insisted on accompanying Chip to Assembly Hall for the team's trip to Springfield. As usual, Soapy kidded everyone in sight and barely got off the bus before the driver closed the door. "Give my best to Jimmy, Chip!" he yelled. "And if there's any way I can help . . . ."

Soapy had even managed to print a copy of the sports section from the Springfield paper off the Internet and handed it to Chip just as the driver was shutting the doors.

The first thing Chip saw was a streamer across the top of the page.

NATIONAL CHAMPS IN
DOUBLE-HEADER TONIGHT
Southwestern Meets Wesleyan—Wilson Plays State

Local basketball fans will have a preview of the Holiday Invitational Tournament tonight at Wilson Arena when three of the competing teams, including the defending champion, Southwestern, meet in a double bill. Southwestern is expected to register its forty-third consecutive victory without too much difficulty since Wesleyan is comparatively weak.

In the nightcap, Wilson may find a hurdle in State University's varsity, which is coming along fast after a slow start.

The page was studded with pictures of Southwestern's talented players surrounding their all-American teammates, Tom Bordon and Reggie Ralk. Chip turned to the next page and found the Wilson University squad featured in a group picture. Directly below was a photo of himself and the following story.

CHIP HILTON
State Sophomore Sensation to Face Wilson Tonight,
WU Out to Stop High-Scoring Marksman

Wilson University is facing two tasks tonight at the arena: protecting its current season victory record and holding Chip Hilton, State's high-scoring sophomore marksman, in check.

TOURNAMENT CRISIS

Hilton has played in four games and has scored 93 points in 69 minutes for an average of 1.5 points per minute. The all-American quarterback is showing the way on the hardcourt just as he did last fall on the gridiron. Reporting late because of football, the blond bomber immediately broke into the starting lineup. He suffered a knee injury at Southwestern (25 points in 24 minutes) a week ago but is reported to be in good shape for the game tonight.

"I hope, I hope," Chip murmured, closing the paper. He rested until the team arrived in Springfield. Right after registering at the hotel, he reported to Rockwell and took a cab to the Tea House.

"Practice is at four o'clock at the arena!" Rockwell warned him. "Be on time. Bring Jimmy with you."

The taxi driver knew exactly where to go and took less than ten minutes to reach Chip's destination. The Tea House was attractively fronted with bamboo and Chinese characters. Chip gave it a quick glance and hurried inside, eager to see his friend.

Inside the dining room, he paused uncertainly. There wasn't a soul in sight. He hesitated and looked around. The interior was exactly as Jimmy had described it. The walls were covered with painted flowers and birds in gaudy colors, and dusty, old-fashioned light fixtures hung from the ceiling, offering little light.

Just as Chip was going to call out, a waiter came forward slowly and bowed. "Is Jimmy here?" Chip asked. "Li Hong Chung?"

The waiter bowed and nodded. "You must mean Chung, Li Hong."

Remembering Dr. Kennedy and his Chinese history class, Chip responded, "Yes, Chung, Li Hong. Thanks."

"Please be seated." The waiter led Chip to a small table and waited until Chip had seated himself. Then he bowed and walked quietly away. He had scarcely passed from Chip's view when the curtain at the back of the room parted and Jimmy came hurrying forward.

"Welcome, Chip. I knew you would come. How about something to eat?"

"Can't, Jimmy. We eat at five o'clock. How is your father?"

The happy expression vanished from Jimmy's face. "Not well, Chip. Everything has gone wrong. Pop has been sick for nearly a month and didn't tell me, and then he had trouble with the cooks and waiters, and most of them left. Besides, business has been terrible. Everything looks pretty hopeless. Mom called and I just had to leave."

Chip gave him Pete's letter. "He misses you, Jimmy. We all miss you. Coach Corrigan and Coach Rockwell want you to come back to school. Isn't there something we can do? Pete said he could help if money would do any good."

"Money would help, but it would just be postponing the inevitable," Jimmy said despondently. "There's a lot more to it than money."

"Couldn't you play tonight?"

"Not a chance, Chip. I've got to forget basketball and school and everything else except my responsibilities as the eldest son."

"I wish I could do something. Maybe I could talk to your father."

"I'd like you to meet Pop, but it would be time thrown away to talk about sports. He detests sports. No, my place is here."

"Your place is in college. Anyway, you can come to the game, can't you? I've got some tickets."

"I can't even do that, Chip. I've got to stay on the job. Not that there's much business."

"I can't see why your brother doesn't run the restaurant. Especially since he likes the restaurant business."

"Tommy could do a wonderful job if Pop would only change his methods. But Tommy will never cooperate as long as Pop won't try to expand the business. That was the cause of the trouble between Tommy and Pop. It's the reason Tommy left home."

"But doesn't he have responsibilities too? Aren't they the same as yours?"

"He has responsibilities, but the eldest son, the first son, is dedicated to carrying on the family name and assuming the leadership in family problems. No, it's up to me and there's no way out."

They sat a long while in silence, as friends often do while seeking the solution to a difficult problem. Chip had been slowed down, but he wasn't about to give up.

"There's got to be a way," he said stubbornly. "Just got to be! Let's talk it over later. Think you could get off to come to the hotel before the team leaves? I know Coach Corrigan wants to see you, and so do all the guys."

Jimmy laughed shortly. "I'll be there. Come on outside, and I'll show you how to get to the arena."

Jimmy stood in the entrance until Chip had passed from sight. Then he turned dejectedly and walked back through the door of the Tea House.

Chip was early. Southwestern had just finished its shooting practice, and the players were joking and sitting along the bench. He glanced at them and sat down to wait for his teammates. While he waited, he thought about Jimmy's problem.

When the State squad arrived, Chip told Rockwell what had transpired at the Tea House and then joined the team. He dressed quickly, eager to get the feel of the court and try his shots. But he didn't have much chance to practice. Several photographers appeared and insisted that he pose for a number of pictures. In the background he could hear the heckling of the Southwestern players.

"Mr. Shotsky in person!"

"The heaver fires again!"

"Yeah, Chip shots by Hilton!"

"A one-man team, that's all!"

Chip was burning, but he ignored the gibes and concentrated on his shots. But every word of ridicule strengthened his resolve to play the game of his life against Wilson. They fired him with an intense desire for another chance at Southwestern. "If we could only meet them in the tournament . . . ," he whispered to himself.

It was hard to take the taunts without fighting back, but Chip concealed the bitterness and kept his head. And it was this control of his emotions that gained him a friend. As he left the floor, a player about his own height and age stopped him. "Hello, Hilton. My name is Greg Moran. I'm captain of the Wilson team. I've been sitting here listening to those Southwestern jerks, and I just had to introduce myself and tell you how much I admire your self-control. I don't think I could have taken it."

"They were just kidding."

"Kidding or not, it wasn't good sportsmanship. Not that you could expect them to be good sports. I know all about that crowd."

Before Moran left, he and Chip became good friends. And when Southwestern ran out on the court to warm up for its game with Wesleyan later that night, Chip and Greg were sitting side by side in the player section like old friends.

During the first half of the game, Chip learned that his new friend was a senior and majoring in engineering. Greg knew Jimmy Chung and all about the Tea House. "Jimmy and I were in the same class in high school and played basketball together. He's a good guy—and really smart."

"He sure is!"

"It would be *something* if he and I lined up against each other tonight."

"Not much chance. He had to go home."

"Oh, no! Why?"

"His father is sick, and he has to take charge of the restaurant." Chip told Greg all about Jimmy's trouble and how badly the team needed him. "But his father is dead set against sports, I guess."

Greg nodded understandingly. "*Now* I remember. Jimmy had a tough time playing when he was in high school. Come to think of it, I believe that was the reason he didn't go to Wilson. Guess he figured he could play basketball at State, but WU was too close to home."

The first half ended then, with Southwestern leading Wesleyan by a score of 42-19. Chip and Greg parted to head for the locker rooms, each wishing the other a good game. Chip couldn't help but compare this kind of hospitality with the reception he and his teammates had received at Southwestern.

And when Chip and his teammates came out on the floor for their pregame warm-up, Chip found it was a different basketball crowd too. The cheerleaders led the home fans in a rousing cheer for State, and the Wilson band even played State's alma mater. The score of the first game was still showing on the board, and Chip saw that the champions had won their forty-third straight game with ease: Southwestern 92, Wesleyan 44.

It looked as if Wilson was going to have an easy time too. It was a solid ball club that used a sharp, short-passing attack and permitted few mistakes. On the defense, Wilson played straight man-to-man. Chip got good shots in the first half. But despite his twenty points, State left the court at the half with Wilson ahead, 47-38.

The Southwestern players had been seated in the first row of seats along the side of the court and stood up to leave the arena for their hotel just as Chip and the rest of the State players left the floor.

"You guys going to drop out of the tournament?" Ralk needled insolently. "It's for college teams! Or didn't you know?"

"We know," Barkley rejoined coolly. "And we'll be there."

"For the first game, maybe," Bordon chimed in. "Why don't you guys try volleyball?"

"That's an idea," Andy Thornhill agreed calmly. "We might. But at least it would be a team that knows something about sportsmanship and would have a few real athletes."

"You wouldn't know how to act," Ralk retorted. "Hey, Hilton! Hey, blond bomber! Keep shootin'! You're bound to make a few if you keep throwing 'em up there!"

Chip said nothing, but once again he was fired up with a grim determination to even the score with Southwestern. "If only we had Jimmy," he murmured fiercely. "We've *got* to get him back!"

CHAPTER 14

We're in the Restaurant Business!

GREG MORAN was a fine basketball player, a good captain, and a sportsman. He possessed a fine shooting eye, and he was having one of the best nights of his career. Greg was the leading scorer of his team and was averaging about twenty-five points per game. At the half he had twenty-two points, and the fans were aware that he had a good chance to break the WU Arena scoring record of fifty-three points. In the second half Greg took up where he had left off in the first and scored five straight points, putting Wilson fourteen points out in front. Kirk Barkley called a time-out, and the State players ringed around Corrigan in front of the State bench.

"I've got four personals, Coach," Barkley said. "I can't stop Moran without fouling."

"All right," Corrigan said briskly. "Switch with Chip. Chip, you take Moran. You've got to stop him."

"Chip will stop him," Speed muttered.

Moran smiled when Chip lined up against him after

the time-out. "I've got new company, huh?" he said, extending his hand.

Chip smiled in return and then sobered. This was for keeps, and State needed this game. He was aware that Greg had scored a lot of points, but he had not given any thought to the shots his new friend used. He found out quickly enough. While Chip was thinking about it, Greg passed off, faked a hard cut, dropped back, and took a return pass. Then, just as Chip would have done, he fired a shot over Chip's head that never touched the rim.

"Sorry 'bout that," Greg said, falling back on the defense.

"You won't get me with that one again," Chip said ruefully.

State was playing well, but Wilson held the fourteen-point lead through the midway mark of the second half. Chip garnered twelve points to bring his total to thirty-two, while Moran had scored another basket and a foul to bring his total to thirty points. The fans were cheering both players now and were keenly aware that Greg and Chip both might break the record.

During the time-out, Corrigan studied the score-board. "It's 71-57," he said worriedly. "Ten minutes left to play and fourteen points behind."

"Better press," Barkley said worriedly. "Try Morris, Reardon, and Bollinger for Andy, Bill, and me. *We're* not getting anywhere."

"Let's change the tempo on them," Corrigan said briskly.

State sent in Sky Bollinger at center, Bradley Gowdy and Speed Morris at the forwards, and Bitsy Reardon and Chip at the guard positions. It was a small team, but it was speedy. Gowdy was the only member of the group who was not exceptionally fast. And it was this tremendous team speed that caused Wilson's downfall.

TOURNAMENT CRISIS

Before the Wilson players could adjust themselves to the change of pace in State's attack, Chip had scored four quick jumpers and slipped Speed the ball for two easy layups. That brought the score to 71-69, and Greg Moran had no choice but to call a Wilson time-out.

"We've got 'em going," Corrigan said breathlessly, glancing at the clock. "Seven minutes to play! Keep it up! Give the ball to Chip. He's hot!"

Corrigan didn't have to stress that; the fans had switched their cheers from Moran to Chip now because Greg had fallen behind in the scoring. Chip had forty points while Greg had *only* thirty-three.

But the fans also knew there was enough time left for State to win the game. And the scoring record was secondary compared to the loss of the game.

State made a lot of mistakes during the next six minutes, but Wilson made more. With the score 88 to 87 in Wilson's favor, Moran called another time-out. Chip had tied the individual scoring record on the last play and now had fifty-three points.

Chip heard the mixed cheering of the fans: encouraging shouts for the home team and the cheers for a new record. But he wasn't interested in records. He wanted his *team* to win the game. This was for the team and State.

Chip checked the game clock as Wilson inbounded the ball. Thirty-four seconds . . . thirty . . . the shot clock was turned off. Bitsy pressed and dove for the ball. But he missed, and Speed and Chip were forced to drop back into their own backcourt to cover for him. The Wilson guards brought the ball up the court, watching the clock to escape the ten-second violation. They also planned to use every possible second left in the game.

WE'RE IN THE RESTAURANT BUSINESS!

The Wilson guards were across the ten-second line and into their frontcourt, and Bitsy had caught up with his opponent.

Chip was playing decoy and so was Speed. Bitsy began to chase the ball. His mad dives and threats had the Wilson players on edge, and they forgot about Speed and Chip. And then it happened!

Speed leaped forward and intercepted the ball with ten seconds left to play. Chip saw it coming and broke for the State basket. He took Speed's toss out in front all alone and dribbled upcourt at full speed, concentrating on the basket. Behind him, he could hear Greg Moran pounding the court, practically breathing down his neck. Then, above the shouts and whoops of the fans, Chip heard Sky Bollinger. "Shoot, Chip! Shoot!"

But Chip didn't shoot. Just as Greg leaped into the air to stop the layup, Chip bounced the ball to Sky on the other side of the basket. Sky was so surprised that he nearly missed the bounce pass. But he caught it and leaped high in the air. But—he missed the shot!

The ball hit the backboard, rebounded, rolled around the rim, and started to fall into the lane. Chip recovered his balance just under the basket, leaped with all his power, and stabbed at the ball. His fingers barely touched the leather, but he flicked the ball back up on the rim. There the ball balanced for a second and then fell through the hoop, just as the buzzer sounded. State had won 89 to 88, and Chip had set a new Wilson University Arena record of fifty-five points.

A casual spectator would have thought State had won the national championship. The players ganged up on Chip, pounding his back and shoulders! Every State player and manager was off the bench and giving hugs and high-fives to anyone in range! The Wilson players weren't far behind, and their first player to reach Chip was Greg Moran.

"Great, Chip! Great! You broke the scoring record. Congratulations on the win too! I'll wait for you right here. We're actually staying at the same hotel."

The photographers and sportswriters were next and walked along with him to the State locker room. There the players staged another celebration.

"Now we're on our way!"

"Great defense, Bitsy!"

"Nice steal, Speed!"

"Some tip, Chip!"

"Atta baby, Sky!"

Sky Bollinger was the most enthusiastic. "Man, would I have been ruined, or *would* I have been ruined if Chip hadn't made that shot? Imagine him passing up a chance to win the game and break the record all on one play and giving me the ball! Guess you guys would've made me walk home if he hadn't made it!"

"It worked out all right," Chip laughed. "Forget it!"

The newspaper writers were still typing their stories on their laptops at the long scorers' table when Chip finished dressing and got back to the court. Greg was talking to some sportswriters, and Chip signaled he'd wait outside in the lobby. Chip liked that Coach Corrigan gave the State postgame interviews. He didn't want to interrupt Greg's meeting with the writer.

A few minutes later Chip ushered Greg into a cab with Speed, Bitsy, and Sky, despite the driver's protests. "We're little guys," Bitsy said lightly. The driver eyed Sky's six feet, nine inches doubtfully but couldn't resist Bitsy's exuberance and smilingly acquiesced.

On the way, Greg took part in the conversation so easily and naturally that he seemed like an old friend.

"What a comeback! You sure caught us by surprise."

"We had Southwestern going too," Sky said. "Or, rather, Chip did."

"We'll get 'em the next time!" Speed added.

"If you play as you played tonight," Greg agreed.

"They're tough though. Tonight was game number forty-three, and they've got three more before the tournament. Coach Habley believes in keeping them busy."

"When do they go to school?" Sky asked.

"They probably all have tutors and real light class loads," Greg replied, laughing.

They arrived at the hotel, then, and Jimmy was waiting. He greeted Greg warmly. Speed, Sky, and Bitsy headed for their rooms while Jimmy, Greg, and Chip went across the street for a milk shake and a sandwich. Jimmy and Greg talked about their old high school days. Chip listened and said nothing about his resolve to get Jimmy back in school. After eating and talking, the three friends walked back to the hotel.

"Good night, guys," Jimmy said. "I've got to wait here for Coach Corrigan. He wants to talk with me before you guys leave early tomorrow morning."

Chip and Jimmy shook hands and promised to keep in touch. The look in Jimmy's eyes was still with Chip when he went to bed. He couldn't sleep. He couldn't get Jimmy's problem out of his mind and tossed until daylight.

When the bus pulled into University Thursday morning, Chip was tired out, but he had worked out a plan to get Jimmy back in school and back on the basketball team. He could hardly wait to get started on the plan and hurried to Pete's Place after his first class.

Pete welcomed him warmly. "Hiya, Chip. Great win last night. Just readin' about the game in the paper. Man, you did yourself proud! Fifty-five points! Wow!"

His happy expression changed. "See Jimmy? How is he?"

"He's fine, Pete, but his heart is just about broken. I've got an idea. I thought about it all night. Jimmy's father is sick and won't be back in the restaurant for a week or so, maybe longer. Tommy Chung is a good restaurant man; Jimmy says he's an expert in the business.

"How's this for an idea? Suppose we could get the restaurant on a paying basis and get Tommy back on the job to take charge? Then Mr. Chung might be willing to let Jimmy come back to school. He might even let him play in the tournament. Sound all right?"

Pete's eyes brightened. "Sounds good! You sure Jimmy would go along with this idea?"

"He hasn't said so, but I think he will. Especially if Tommy will come home and help."

"You think the father would let Jimmy come back to school?"

"Yes, I do. Education is especially important to the Chinese, Pete."

"Well, count on me! Where do we start?"

"I can't get away from school and practice, and that's where you come in. If you can get Tommy down here, so we can talk to him, we'll be able to find out what we need and where to start. Jimmy says Tommy has a lot of wonderful plans for the restaurant and that was the reason he left home."

"You got the address? Good! You know what I'm going to do? I'm going to get in my car right now and drive to Chicago and bring Tommy back with me, dead or alive! I'll have him back here tomorrow. You call and tell him I'm coming. If he's any kind of a brother at all, he'll be glad to help Jimmy. You want action? You got action! Right?

"Now listen, Chip. Jimmy is important to me and Pete's Place. Jimmy is important for his own sake, but he's also important to the business. See you tomorrow, and I'll have Tommy Chung with me. Positively!"

Pete was back on Friday, and Tommy Chung was with him. "All set, Chip. Meet Tommy. He quit his job. If this idea of yours doesn't click, he's going to work for me."

Tommy was about as tall as Jimmy but not athletic. He had the same dark, steady eyes and friendly expression. Pete had evidently briefed his passenger thoroughly, and Tommy was ready and willing.

"I want to do my part," he said, spreading his hands. "If Jimmy needs help, I'm ready. However, it's a big job."

"You don't know me and Chip!" Pete boasted.

Tommy smiled briefly. "I know my father," he said significantly. "He's an extremely decided man."

"But he'll change if we can get the business booming, won't he? That's the big problem facing the family right now, isn't it?"

Tommy nodded. "That is the most vital problem, yes. But there are other family matters that present difficulty too."

"What's the next move?" Pete asked impatiently. "We haven't got much time."

Chip agreed. "The next thing is for you and Tommy to talk everything over and agree on what changes are needed in the restaurant setup and what the cost will be."

Tommy nodded his head vigorously. "A few changes will be necessary. It is mostly the need for a change of policy. The location is excellent. The outside of the building can be fixed with a little paint, and the dining room requires nothing but some white paint to cover up all the colors of the rainbow on the walls. Oh, and better lighting. Mostly cosmetic things."

"How about the kitchen equipment?"

"It is excellent," Tommy said proudly. "The ranges and tables and ovens and refrigerators are as good as you will find anywhere. And the kitchen is large and clean. No improvements are needed there."

"What about changing the name? Won't that be important?"

"Definitely! I've been thinking about a name for a long time, and I think any change should be small. I like the 'New China Tea House,' out of respect for Pop. And, because we're located right off the Wilson campus, we'll want the menu in English, but we'll keep the Mandarin too. And maybe add a take-out portion to the menu. Pete has also mentioned some advertising in the community."

"Now what?" Pete asked impatiently.

"Well," said Chip. "finals are finishing, and Christmas vacation starts tomorrow. If you and Tommy can be ready, Soapy and I can get to Springfield by tomorrow. Remember, we have the game tonight. We'll just go home to Valley Falls a few days later. Can you make it, Pete?"

"Sure! I'm in this all the way. I'll be ready. But what about your holidays at home with your parents?"

"We'll be there with time to spare. Suppose you and Tommy talk everything over this afternoon, and Soapy and I'll finalize our ideas before tomorrow."

"That's the kind of action I like," Pete said. "Tommy can help me this afternoon and go to the game with you tonight. Another thing, this extra traveling is going to cost you and Soapy a lot of money. I'll finance that item and figure it's money well spent if we can get Jimmy back. OK with you?"

WE'RE IN THE RESTAURANT BUSINESS!

"Thanks, Pete. But that's not necessary. We'll get there."

Pete wasn't budging. "You'll get there safe and sound with me. And with my money! I'm driving, so be ready to leave before dawn! This is an investment in my business. Got it? Good. I'll pick you and Soapy up at your dorm."

Chip arrived early for practice that afternoon. It was an unusual procedure for the day of a game, but Coach Corrigan felt it was necessary because the players were leaving for Christmas vacation right after the game that night. Rockwell was on hand to discuss scouting reports of the teams that had been invited to the tournament.

After the usual walk-through of the offense and defense and thirty minutes of shooting, Corrigan talked about the game with Cathedral that night and finished with an outline of plans for the tournament. "We'll have a few days off for the Christmas holiday, and that will be a well-deserved break from classes and practice. We'll report back here on Sunday, December 26, at 10 A.M. to get in a good, short practice. We'll then leave that afternoon for Springfield. Now let's take Cathedral tonight and then start thinking about winning the tournament."

After practice, Chip hurried down to the locker room and cornered Murph Kelly. "Murph, can you have one of the managers pack Jimmy Chung's uniform for the tournament? I'm going to have him back in time to play."

Chip had lots of things to do that afternoon. He met Soapy and urged him to pack that afternoon. "We won't have much time after we close up tonight at work."

"Why? Where we going?"

"Springfield! We leave first thing in the morning! You, Pete, Tommy Chung, and I are going into the restaurant business. For a few days anyway!"

CHAPTER 15

'Tis the Season for Giving

HOLIDAY VACATIONS! Nothing electrifies a college campus more than the ending of finals and an upcoming holiday! Thousands of State students had remained in University to see the Statesmen defeat Cathedral, 74-69. It was a perfect beginning to their holiday break! Chip Hilton's name was on the lips of every basketball fan who talked about State's third-straight victory and the thirty-six points the blond bomber had scored for the winning cause.

Chip had been hot again and had scored all thirty-six points in just twenty-nine minutes. But as soon as the game was over, Mike Terring examined Chip's knee. "Yep, it's swollen. You need some more rest before this tournament. Coach and I have already talked. You're to take Monday and Tuesday off—that's right, no practice—and then report to me on Wednesday morning for another look. Coach wants you in good shape for that tournament. Now beat it." Mike Terring grinned.

Chip plunged right back into the problem of the Tea House when he and Soapy climbed into Pete's back seat at five o'clock the next morning.

"Greg Moran is meeting us at the Wilsonian Inn, and then we're going to get Jimmy in a huddle and get started. I worked out a job assignment for each of us yesterday afternoon."

As Soapy nodded off to sleep, he remarked, "I hope Greg has breakfast waiting for us."

"It's a big step for Jimmy," Tommy said thoughtfully. "It will be necessary for him to discuss these plans with our father. Right now, it's important that I present myself to my father and beg his forgiveness for my long absence."

None of Tommy's listeners attempted to advise Tommy about his family obligations. Shortly afterward, Pete's three passengers quieted and tried to get as much sleep as possible.

Greg Moran was waiting in the lobby of the Wilsonian Inn. Greg knew Tommy slightly, and the two shook hands. Then Chip introduced him to his other friends and explained their mission.

"We're out to get Jimmy back in school and on the team, and we need your help."

"You've got it. What can I do?"

"Nothing right now, but we'll all get together just as soon as Tommy has seen Jimmy and his father. We're to meet them at the restaurant at two o'clock."

"Hey, are you guys staying here? Stay at my house. The Moran house is the best place in town to stay!" Greg said, laughing. "Move in with us. We have lots of room."

Pete was impressed with Greg's hospitality but had to decline since they would be working long hours at the restaurant.

TOURNAMENT CRISIS

After the two restaurant entrepreneurs, as Soapy called Pete and Tommy, checked into their rooms at the Wilsonian Inn, Tommy cut across the campus to the Tea House, and Greg went home for awhile.

Greg returned shortly before two o'clock, and Pete drove them to the restaurant. Jimmy and Tommy were expecting them.

Inside the restaurant, everyone surrounded Jimmy, shaking his hand and making a fuss over him. Jimmy was upset. Despite the hearty welcome, Chip could sense the distress in Jimmy's eyes and voice. But the plan had gone too far to draw back now, and Chip took the initiative. "How's your father?"

"He's pretty sick, Chip. I guess he won't be able to work for a long time."

"Tommy tell you about our plan?"

"Yes, Chip. I don't know what to do."

"Only one thing *to* do. According to tradition, you're the head of the family now, and it's your responsibility to take care of the business. You're supposed to make it a success, right?"

"Yes . . ."

"All right, we're here to help you! I've got everything planned. We start Monday on the outside, painting and changing the name, like Tommy wants, to the New China Tea House. Everyone gets a paintbrush and pitches in. Pete is in charge of that. On Tuesday we clean up the inside and cover all the different colors with white paint. Pete is in charge of that too."

"But where is the money coming from?"

Pete elbowed Soapy and Greg aside and, with elaborate gestures, pulled a huge roll of bills out of his pocket. "Look what I found in my cash register," he said grandly.

"*This* is where the working capital is coming from. And if we need more, I can get it!"

"But maybe we can't pay it back."

"No buts! You don't have to pay it back unless this plan of Chip's goes over. If it doesn't, I'll chalk the whole thing up to experience."

"It isn't going to cost much," Chip added. "Greg and I are going to work out a sales plan and the advertising program—"

"Excuse me, Chip," Greg interrupted, "I can really help in that department. Bob Chandler is the school's sports information director, and he's engaged to my sister. He said he'd like to help too. He knows every sportswriter in town!"

"That's great!" Chip said quickly.

"And," Greg continued, "he can get us a break for ads on the sports pages, and that will fall right in line with your plan to make the New China Tea House the sports center of Springfield."

"Sports center?" Jimmy echoed weakly, with his face growing pale.

Chip nodded quickly. "Sure! Coach Rockwell told me he would arrange for State's basketball team to eat lunch and dinner here during the tournament. Then we can work on the other teams and line them up for the same thing. We'll fill the place!"

Greg laid a hand on Chip's arm. "Sorry, Chip. I don't like to be butting in all the time, but Bob's in charge of arranging the housing and meals for all the teams, and he'll be thrilled to have a restaurant so close to the campus. I'll call him right now, OK?"

"Wow!" Chip assented. "That's great!"

"Wait a minute," Soapy chimed in. "How about tickets to campus concerts or the community theater?

Couldn't the New China Tea House be the ticket center for the community events and activities?"

"Sure!" Greg said. "Bob is looking for a place to make them available during the tournament. Keep talking. I'll be right back!"

Chip carried on again. "Jimmy, you, Tommy, and Pete will do the buying and set up the kitchen. That's your expertise. Soapy will find a staff to wait tables, even if he has to use Biggie Cohen, Red Schwartz, and every State student from Valley Falls. He might even get Chet Stewart's Big Reds high school basketball team up here! And it won't cost anything except their meals. Don't worry. You can't miss! We're not going to let you miss!"

"But—"

"No *buts!* Now you and Tommy go back home and tell your father you've got some new ideas and you're sure they will be successful."

Jimmy nodded uncertainly. "All right, Chip. Er— could Tommy and I speak to you privately?"

"Sure. Come on, I'll walk you partway home. Soapy, can you wait here for Greg and Pete? I'll be right back."

As soon as they were out of earshot, Jimmy began. "Chip, I'm worried about this whole thing. Pop wouldn't talk to Tommy this morning, and Tommy doesn't know what to do. He's thinking about going back to Chicago. Then there's the restaurant. Pop is dead set in his ways and ideas."

"I know, Jimmy. But this is the chance you and Tommy both have wanted. And with all the help we've got, I'm sure it will go over the top. If it doesn't, there won't be much loss. You're losing money now. Why not try it?

"As far as Tommy is concerned, I think he should stay here and show his father what he can do. Then, if it doesn't work and you can't come back to school, Tommy can take your place with Pete."

Chip gripped Jimmy tightly by the arm. "Tommy deserves a chance too. This is it."

"All right," Jimmy agreed reluctantly. "We'll give it a try."

Chip could scarcely restrain a shout of relief. "Good. We've got five or six days before the teams begin to arrive for the tournament and almost two weeks after that before school starts. You haven't withdrawn from State, so you're still a full-time student, your grades are excellent, and you're still on the team roster and eligible to play."

"Might as well forget the basketball," Jimmy said shortly. "All I hope is that you get another chance at Southwestern."

Chip explained that he and Soapy had to go home that afternoon but that they would be back Monday and ready to go to work. "Pete is staying over the weekend. He'll meet you at the restaurant tonight. He's a good man and knows the business. Guess I don't have to tell either of you that."

Chip, Soapy, Pete, and Greg spent the rest of the afternoon going over further plans for the New China Tea House, and by the time Chip and Soapy had to leave for their flight to Valley Falls, they had covered every detail. Greg was enthusiastic and promised to get half of the local Wilson students lined up for Chip's phone campaign. "I can get a lot of local students to work too," he said enthusiastically. "I know just about every waiter and waitress in school. Most of them are looking for something to do during the holidays. Don't you worry about that little detail."

"Only two requirements," Soapy warned. "They've got to be willing to work and the girls have to look like Mitzi."

"Who's Mitzi?" Greg asked with a puzzled look.

"Ignore Soapy, Greg. He's just starting to realize he won't see Mitzi for almost three weeks."

"Not true, my fine Christmas friend," Soapy countered, smiling mysteriously.

On the plane, Chip settled himself comfortably in his seat, anticipating a good rest, but he should have known better. Soapy was curious, wide awake, and full of questions. "Chip, you asleep? Weren't we lucky to get our tickets so cheap? Think we'll get a meal on this flight? What's this phone campaign Greg was talking about? You asleep?"

Chip gave in to Soapy's excitement. "We're going to make lists of people to call and tell about the New China Tea House. Faculty, local students, residents, and all kinds of groups and organizations."

"Good idea. Most of the teams will be in Springfield for New Year's even. Some, like State, will be spending Christmas in town, depending on their travel plans. You figuring on anything special?"

"That's your department. Get busy and make some plans. I'm going to sleep."

Two tired college sophomores alighted in a blinding snowstorm at the Valley Falls Regional Airport. There wasn't a taxi in sight. "True to form," Soapy grumbled. "C'mon, let's call Speed. He's the closest to your house. Wonder what your mom's got baked for the holidays? Christmas cookies? Pumpkin pies? I better stay at your house tonight."

Mary Hilton was awake as soon as the three pairs of feet stomped up on the porch. The familiar hallway light shone with welcome, and she hurried downstairs to gather the boys into the warm family room.

'TIS THE SEASON FOR GIVING

Over hot cocoa and cookies, Chip outlined his plans to get Jimmy Chung back in school. His mom was in complete agreement with his intense desire to help a friend. They each confirmed that the holiday season was all about giving and helping others.

Speed and Soapy called their parents and spent the night inside the warmth of the long-familiar Hilton home, just as they had for years when growing up in Valley Falls. Soapy was the last of the three friends to clomp up the stairs to Chip's room. He had "something important" to discuss with Chip's mom.

Chip had a wonderful time the next day. Soapy and Speed, eager to go home to see their families, had gotten up early and quietly left. When Chip and his mom went to church later that morning, the air was still frigid, but the skies were a clear blue, and the sun playfully sparkled on the snow.

After lunch, Chip borrowed his mom's car and drove Speed and Soapy down to the Sugar Bowl. All of the old crowd was there, standing on the sidewalk just outside the entrance and scanning the large poster in the window. Most of them were curious about the tournament.

"You see the draw, Chip?" someone asked. "Petey hung it in the window. State meets Dane University in the first round. Know anything about them?"

"Not much," Chip said, moving up to the window to study the draw sheet.

TOURNAMENT CRISIS

HOLIDAY INVITATIONAL DRAW

FIRST ROUND	QUARTER-FINALS	SEMIFINALS	FINALS

Midwestern

*Afternoon
Mon. Dec. 27*

*Night
Tues. Dec. 28*

Deacon Univ.

Southwestern

*Night
Thurs. Dec. 30*

A & M

Kingwood (85)

*Night
Wed. Dec. 29*

*Night
Mon. Dec. 27*

Wilson Univ. (86)

**FINALS
NIGHT**
*8:15
Friday
Dec. 31*

Templeton

*Afternoon
Mon. Dec. 27*

*Night
Wed. Dec. 29*

Brant

College of the West

*Night
Thurs. Dec. 30*

Southeastern U.

Dane University

*Night
Tues. Dec. 28*

*Night
Mon. Dec. 27*

State

"They gave A & M a bye, Chip," said Speed. "How come?"

"They were champions of the conference last year, Speed. Guess that's the reason. Hmmm, Dane. Rock said they played a possession game."

Speed pulled his copy of Henry Rockwell's scouting notes out of his pocket. "That's right," he added. "They play slow and make few mistakes, and they've got a big center . . . six-ten and good."

"Southwestern is seeded number one," someone behind Chip said. "They as good as everyone says? That's the only team anyone around here talks about."

"Yeah, Chip, you think it's the greatest team of all time?"

Chip swung around and faced the group. "Hold it," he said, laughing. "What am I supposed to be? How would *I* know whether or not it's the greatest team of all time?"

"You played against them and you got twenty-five points—"

"Yeah," Speed interrupted, "and he got decked too! And good! They have a good team, but they play dirtball. And no team is great that plays dirty!"

CHAPTER 16

There Was Something Magical

TOMMY CHUNG had no experience with a paintbrush, but there was artistry in his hands! The large sign proudly hanging in front of his father's restaurant had been beautifully transformed and looked as if it had been designed exclusively for the New China Tea House.

Chip and Soapy arrived in Springfield at ten o'clock on Monday morning and took a taxi directly to the restaurant. Tommy had completed the red and gold sign by that time and was helping Jimmy, Pete, and Greg on the front of the building. The newcomers sat in the cab, too surprised to move, and viewed the transformation. The frame structure had absorbed the first coat of white paint beautifully, and the big sign with its red and gold letters looked clean and inviting.

Pete spotted them from his high perch on a ladder and bellowed a greeting. "C'mon. We got work to do! Hope you brought some work clothes."

That shocked them to life. They paid the cab driver

and hustled to the front entrance. A poster announcing that the New China Tea House was closed for renovations was tacked on the door. Inside, two men from the phone company were installing phone lines. Chip and Soapy changed clothes in the restroom and hurried out to join the workers.

"How's it look?" Pete demanded.

Before either could answer, Jimmy interrupted. "We're getting a phone!"

"Greg's got the tickets all set," Tommy added.

"That's right," Greg said proudly. "Got some friends lined up to do the phoning too. They'll be here tomorrow afternoon. And, Chip, Bob thinks we ought to run some ads in all the papers when we're ready to go. And another thing! He wants to get some classy menus printed up. He and Pete have started the design already, and Tommy and Jimmy will compose the Mandarin and English translations. Bob'll be over tomorrow afternoon. Says we can count on practically all of the teams eating here."

"C'mon, you guys!" Pete growled. "We've got two more sides to paint and a second coat to put on. Today! We gotta get the outside all finished before sundown."

They did it . . . and before sundown! And then they started on the interior. First they piled up all the tables and chairs and spread newspapers and drop cloths over the floor. Then they removed all the plants and other decorations. Chip was dead tired, and Soapy and Greg were practically tripping over their own feet in their fatigue, but they didn't quit. They tackled the ceiling with rollers dipped in soft blue paint and finished the job at midnight.

When the last roll of paint covered the center of the ceiling—without a word, almost as if by command—they sat down on the floor and viewed the results of their labor. Then they looked at one another and burst into hysterical laughter. Their hands and faces were spattered with light blue and imperial yellow paint, and Soapy's hair had changed from a bright, monochromatic red to a speckled, motley hue of red, yellow, and blue.

They cleaned up as best they could and called it a day.

They made real progress on Tuesday. They finished the main dining room walls in imperial yellow before lunch and started on the trim. When Bob Chandler showed up, Chip stopped long enough to get acquainted and to outline his plans. Chandler was as enthusiastic about the project as Greg and assumed full responsibility for the menus, the publicity, and the designation of the New China Tea House as the food center for the teams entered in the tournament.

"It's as good as done," he said quietly. "Another thing! The school is sponsoring a luncheon for the tournament sportswriters; it's scheduled for Friday at noon. The tournament treasurer will pick up the tab, and it will give you a chance to sell the writers on the New China Tea House. Can you handle it?"

Jimmy, perched on the top rung of the ladder and painting the trim around the main dining room door, nodded his head so emphatically that he nearly fell! "Sure! We can handle it!"

A little later some college girls Greg knew appeared and *all* work immediately ceased. This time Soapy nearly fell off the ladder. Greg introduced everyone, and for the first time, Chip had *too* much help.

He explained that the idea was to make up a list of organizations, students, faculty, and residents who might be interested in special lunches or dinners. Then the girls would call them and tell them about the New China Tea House. Some of the college girls were also waitresses, and they gathered around Tommy since he was going to serve as headwaiter and banquet manager.

"How about *me?*" Soapy demanded. "I've got to have help with *my* project. I can't handle a big Christmas and New Year's party all by myself."

"I can take care of that," Greg said. "Wilson's cheer-leading squad can help you. They're around anyway since we're in the tournament, so let's put them to work!"

Everything seemed to click, and when Greg offered to drive Chip back to University Tuesday evening so he wouldn't have to take the train, the New China Tea House was just about ready to open its doors for business on Wednesday.

The staff was in fairly good shape. Pete's brother had taken over for him in the restaurant in University until the end of the tournament, and he and Jimmy were in full charge of the kitchen. A few of the old kitchen workers had returned when they saw the rejuvenated setup, and Tommy had selected a number of the student waiters and waitresses to help in the dining room.

The transformation was unbelievable, and now the stage was set for the vital part of Chip's plan.

When Greg and Chip reached University at eight o'clock, they went directly to Jeff. The plan was for Greg to spend the night, sleeping in Soapy's empty bed, and then return to Springfield early Wednesday morning in time for basketball practice. Greg was asleep almost as soon as he fell backward on the bed, but Chip quietly headed to Grayson's.

He handled most of the work piled up in the stockroom and then covered for Soapy at the fountain until closing. He also made some calls and found a substitute to work for Soapy while they were at the tournament in Springfield.

First thing the next morning, Chip walked up to the medical center where Dr. Terring gave him the green light for practice. In Assembly Hall, Corrigan drilled the team until twelve o'clock and then excused the players until three o'clock.

Chip caught up with the Rock just as he was about to go into the basketball office. "Coach, can I talk to you?" Chip made it a point to tell Henry Rockwell all about the progress in Springfield.

"Jimmy'll play, Coach," Chip said confidently. "Wait until Mr. Chung sees the new plan in operation and finds out Tommy can handle the restaurant."

Chip took a nap in his room at Jeff and was refreshed and raring to go at the afternoon practice.

After the workout, he completely caught up on his work at Grayson's. When he left, everyone gave him a royal send-off.

"Bring back that big crystal basketball!"

"Watch out for Southwestern!"

"We'll be watching you on TV!"

Speed was waiting for him at Jeff, all packed and eager to help Chip finish gathering his stuff. "It's a great feeling, Chip! Imagine, we're in the big tournament."

Chip was busily pulling out dresser drawers and turning jacket and jeans pockets inside out. Speed watched curiously.

"What are you looking for?"

"That newspaper clipping about Jimmy. The write-up about him from the paper."

"Maybe it's in one of your books."

Chip searched through the books on his desk and found the article in his Chinese history text. "Good! Had me worried."

"What are you going to do with that?"

Chip explained that it was an important bit of ammunition he was accumulating for Jimmy's father. "Going to be all ready for him," he said, grinning happily. "Let's go."

"This is going to be my first Christmas away from home," Speed said ruefully.

"Me, too," Chip said, "but it's worth it."

Soapy met them in Springfield the next morning and reported what had happened at the grand opening. "It was great Chip! I never saw anything like it. Man, this is going to be some day! If Jimmy's father isn't sold on this deal, he wouldn't even appreciate the finest restaurant in . . . in . . . Paris! Oh! You oughta see Greg and me in our white coats. Spiffeee! We're Tommy's junior headwaiters. Impressive, huh?" Soapy grinned. A few specks of imperial yellow still highlighted his carrot top.

It *was* fun. But it was for keeps too. Jimmy's and Tommy's faces showed the strain, but there was happiness in their eyes and in their voices when they greeted Chip.

Coach Corrigan, Coach Rockwell, and the State team arrived early and were given a special table in a corner of the main dining room. Sportswriters were standing around in small groups, talking to players and coaches from the different teams. Chip excused himself and went to look for Pete. He found him in the kitchen, working away quietly and efficiently. Pete grunted a welcome and kept right on going.

Jimmy and Tommy stopped their work for a second, and Jimmy clutched Chip's arm and shook him gently. "Business is great, Chip. I think it's going to work."

"I've always dreamed of this," Tommy said enthusiastically. "You're a genius, Chip."

"That's a laugh."

"I mean it. It was your ideas and your perseverance and determination that sold us. We'll never forget it."

"How's your father?"

"Much better. He expects to come to work the first of the week."

"Could I see him before Monday?"

Jimmy shook his head. "I'm afraid not, Chip. It wouldn't be wise."

"Then I'll see him here first thing Monday morning."

When Chip returned to the dining room, several other teams had arrived; the room was really filling up! Bob Chandler was introducing coaches and writers and players to one another. After lunch, the teams remained seated and various coaches stood to talk about their teams and the tournament. And while they were speaking, the customers kept pouring in.

Coach Corrigan wanted to talk to Jimmy, so Chip took him out in the kitchen where the two brothers were working side by side. Jimmy was embarrassed. "I'm sorry I had to leave without seeing you, Coach, but I couldn't help it."

"By the looks of this, it's understandable, Jimmy. I spoke with your professors, and they tell me you completed all your work *and* your exams for the term. How'd you do that?"

"Well, there wasn't much business, so I had plenty of time. My profs were very helpful. I took all my books with me to study at the restaurant and used the computers at the public library to E-mail assignments. My finals were all take-home examinations anyway, so that was no problem. All I had to do was sleep fast!"

"Good for you, Jimmy. By the way, you made the Dean's List—I checked it just before we came up here.

Congratulations. I want you to know that by NCAA rules and State's rules, you're still eligible, and we're counting on you to play. But, we need you in shape. Can you make practice this afternoon? We want to win this tournament, and you can help us do it."

"Physically, I'm in shape, Coach. The military taught me that. Ever since I left school, I've worked out after closing up the restaurant each night. On Monday and Tuesday when Chip came up, he put me through the paces, and Soapy's begun drilling me in the offensive and defensive plans. He also brought me the tournament scouting notes and is making me practice with him at the YMCA after we close up." Jimmy smiled. "Soapy is a very persuasive guy.

"However," Jimmy shook his head regretfully, "it's impossible for me to come to practice while my father is ill. I must stay here at the restaurant whenever we are open."

Tommy had stood silently at his brother's side but now inched forward. "Late afternoons are slow, Jimmy. There is no need for both of us to be here. You're doing everything you can for Pop. Go ahead and go. You can still attend practice. I insist, Jimmy."

"That would be great, Jimmy," Corrigan agreed as he turned toward the dining room to leave. "I'll expect you there." He turned back around to face the two brothers. "Chip tells me your father may be back on the job on Monday. That will be just in time for the tournament."

"I wish I could share Chip's confidence," Jimmy said, smiling gently. "I don't know what I would have done without him."

"I don't know what we'd do without him either," Jim Corrigan said, smiling and slapping Chip on the back.

TOURNAMENT CRISIS

Everything after that was a blur! So many things happened on Thursday and Friday that Chip couldn't keep track of anything. State practiced and there were the inevitable pictures and interviews with the writers and then watching the other teams practice and then heading back to the New China Tea House.

The holiday clinic for the kids on Friday morning was a tremendous success! When Chip took to the floor at ten o'clock, the lower seating section of Wilson Arena was packed with parents ready to watch their kids. Elementary kids, middle schoolers, high school athletes, all there to receive a new Christmas basketball and some excellent instruction from the college coaches and players attending the tournament. As Chip worked on skills with one of the elementary-age groups, he remembered all the fun he'd had the previous summer at Camp All-America. Rock was right—there was something magical about working with kids!

That evening, Jim Corrigan and the Rock took a group of players from the tournament to Wilson General Hospital to sing Christmas carols. As the players, dressed as Santa's helpers, moved from floor to floor and from room to room, Chip missed his mom more than he thought possible. But Soapy's completely unselfconscious, loud, off-key notes made Chip smile and kept him from dwelling too much on thoughts of home. On the pediatrics floor, one small boy with large brown eyes looked up in amazement and whispered, "You're the biggest elves I've ever seen!" Chip's heart lightened.

Once back at the hotel, he called his mom to wish her a Merry Christmas, but all he got was his mom's voice on the answering machine.

Probably at church still. I'll try her later. But Chip fell asleep before he could try again, and before he knew it, Christmas morning had arrived, and with it came a new light dusting of snow. Chip threw back the covers, leaped out of bed, and called Valley Falls. Again, all he got was the machine. Disappointed, he left a Christmas greeting and then showered and began to dress. Where was Soapy?

Chip was tugging his red Christmas sweater over his head when Soapy banged on the door. "Merry Christmas! Merry Christmas!" As soon as Chip opened the door, Soapy was pulling on Chip's arm, half dragging him to the door. "C'mon! Grab your jacket and let's go!" In the hall Chip could see Speed and a bunch of his other teammates looking perplexed.

"Beats us," Speed said, shrugging. "He's been all over this hotel, rounding us up, and it's not even eight o'clock! It's supposed to be some kind of surprise!"

The teammates bundled up and braved the cold for five blocks; Soapy, naturally, was in the lead and encouraged them: "Hurry up!"

As they turned the last corner, the New China Tea House came into view. Chip was surprised that the lights were already on inside the lobby. As they marched up the walk, the strains of "Silent Night" reached their ears, calling to them. Inside the main dining room, the lights were off. But a six-foot tall Christmas tree stood proudly in the corner, its white lights shimmering festively against the brightly painted yellow walls. And gathered on all sides with Coach Corrigan and Coach Rockwell were the moms and dads and sisters and brothers of the stunned young men who had followed good old Soapy Smith to their surprise.

And what a surprise! As the players embraced their families, the holiday spirit grew to a beautiful intensity. Mary Hilton's sweet laughter filled Chip's heart, and he came to realize home was not a place—home was wherever she and his friends and their families were. And Soapy? Soapy was rewarded doubly for organizing the surprise. Beside his parents and younger sister stood a very proud Mitzi Savrill, swinging a sprig of mistletoe.

In the afternoon the players who weren't practicing met at the restaurant to watch the game between Southwestern and College of the West in Chicago on TV. Bob Chandler had located the set somewhere, and it had been temporarily installed for the pleasure of the athletes.

Several writers joined the group and entered into the spirit of the rejuvenation of the New China Tea House. "What's the big idea?" they queried. "What happened to the original Tea House?"

"Whose idea is this?"

"Why all the help from the college kids?"

But those in the know were saying nothing, and that added to the suspense and fun of the whole experience.

Meanwhile, the game was on the screen, and several strangers were keeping notes on the tables. "This could be a preview of the finals right here next Friday night," someone said.

Soapy couldn't take that. "Except for one thing," he added. "State will be one of the teams."

"State? They haven't got the horses. It's a one-man team. Haven't got a thing except Hilton."

"Haven't got the horses? State will outrun and outshoot any team in the country. Wait and see!"

"I'll wait."

The game action intensified then, and the conversation stilled except for occasional remarks.

"They're a rough outfit."

"You see that? Wasn't that a foul?"

THERE WAS SOMETHING MAGICAL

"Things look different on TV."

Chip concentrated on the screen, oblivious to the remarks, eager to verify the weakness he suspected: Southwestern's inability to play a wide-open, slam-bang, individual game.

It was a rough game to work, and the officials barely held it in check. College of the West was one of the best teams in the country and gave Southwestern a fight. But the champions had too much poise and won with a score of 78-71.

The announcer summarized the scoring and concluded with an overview of Southwestern's season. "Southwestern winds up its pretournament season with a great string of forty-seven straight victories over a two-year period. The Holiday Invitational champions are seeking their forty-eighth victory Tuesday night at Springfield when they take top billing in the feature game. The final night has been sold out for weeks. The preliminary game brings together Southeastern, seeded number four, and the winner of the Monday night game between Dane University and State, seeded sixth and tenth, respectively."

That broke up the afternoon excitement, and Chip and Soapy joined Jimmy and Tommy in the kitchen. The brothers were studying a sports page. "See this, Chip?" Jimmy asked. "See this write-up on Southwestern?"

WILSON TECH COACH LAUDS CHAMPIONS
Southwestern "Team without a Weakness"

Springfield (AP)

Southwestern figures to become the first team to win the Holiday Invitational Tournament three times in a row.

TOURNAMENT CRISIS

Southwestern plays College of the West in Chicago this afternoon and then boards a flight for Springfield, where it's confident of stretching its successive winning streak (providing Southwestern wins this afternoon) to fifty straight. This will come at the expense of at least three teams in the Holiday Invitational and repeat last year's triumph in the process.

No Weakness

"Southwestern is a team without a weakness," Bill Todd, Wilson University coach, declared yesterday while preparing for the tournament. "Coach Jeff Habley has welded five great stars into an organization that carries the mantle of greatness as naturally as most teams wear warm-up jackets."

Habley and his twelve-man varsity squad will arrive in Springfield tonight. The team will work out Monday morning at the Wilson Arena. It's a shame the tournament committee didn't think of charging admission to the practice. It would be a sellout!

"Well?" Jimmy demanded.

"It's a great article," Chip said, choosing his words carefully. "And Southwestern's a great team, but we can beat them."

Chip paused, eyed Jimmy appraisingly, and continued slowly. "Some team is going to beat Southwestern, Jimmy, and I want to play on the team that does it. We're all counting on you to help us do it."

Jimmy swallowed hard. "I'd do anything for you and the team, Chip. You know that! But a person of Chinese ancestry has responsibilities an American can't understand."

THERE WAS SOMETHING MAGICAL

To this point, Tommy hadn't said a word. Now he struck his fist sharply on the table and eyed Jimmy fiercely. "An *American* can't understand?" he echoed. "When you speak of an American, you are speaking of yourself. When will *you* learn that America is your country and not China? You were *born* in America, *not* in China! You're an *American!*"

CHAPTER 17

Have a Friend, Be a Friend

SOAPY'S CHRISTMAS PARTY was a great success! The Wilson University cheerleaders, made up of both guys and girls, had gone all out and arranged for music and decorations. Soapy's tree stood proudly in the corner of the Chinese restaurant, an interesting mixture of East and West. Bob Chandler, who believed in big promotions, succeeded in getting the Tournament Committee to finance the cost of the party for the guests of honor, the tournament players.

Soapy and Greg acted as hosts, introducing the players one by one under the spotlight. They then introduced the girls and guys from Wilson to the players from the various universities. Jimmy and Pete and the kitchen staff were bustling around, preparing platters of meats and rice and vegetables and salads and snacks. Tommy's staff kept replenishing the tables on both sides of the Christmas tree corner with food.

Chip enjoyed the party until ten o'clock. Then he and Speed went back to the hotel with Mary Hilton and

Mr. and Mrs. Morris. The two families visited for an hour or so, and then Chip and Speed headed to their rooms.

It took Chip a long time to go to sleep. His heart was filled with thoughts of the great friendships he had made and the sacrifices Pete, Greg, and Bob Chandler were making for a friend who needed help. And then he thought of the wonderful spirit of the Wilson students who had pitched in to help their friend, Greg Moran. Chip wasn't sure of the wording, but he *was* sure that the actions of all the people who had worked to make the New China Tea House successful must prove the old axiom: To have a friend, be a friend. And then he thought of the expression on Soapy's face as Soapy watched the guys greeting their families. That was what he was still thinking about when he fell asleep.

All of the families attended church together that Sunday morning, and that afternoon, Coach Corrigan and Henry Rockwell held a two-hour chalk talk. Rockwell had more photocopied scouting notes on all the teams in the bottom half of the draw sheet, but he devoted most of his remarks to State's first opponent, Dane University. "We'll take 'em one at a time," he said, smiling confidently.

Coach Corrigan interrupted him for a moment. "Men, Coach Rockwell has notes on every team in the tournament. Naturally, both of us will see every game and try to get as much information as possible on the teams we're going to beat. But we both think you should do your own scouting. So we'll expect you to watch every game played by the teams in our bracket. OK, Rock."

"That's right," Rockwell added. "In order to do a little better job, it might be wise for you to concentrate on individual players—players you may be matched up against. Study his face, his shirt number, and his personal techniques. For example, does he turn his head on the defense? Does he play his opponent or the ball? Does he try for interceptions? Does he switch well? When and where does he foul? Some players never foul an opponent until they are sure he is going to shoot.

"On the offense, does he shoot from outside? Does he dribble a lot? Is he a good passer? From what area on the court does he score? What does he do *without* the ball? Does he screen, pick, or set up blocks? Is he a basket hanger? What does he do on the fast break?

"There's a lot more, of course, but that gives you a pretty good idea what to look for. Coach Corrigan and I will scout the offense and defense and special-team tactics. Any questions?"

Rockwell then briefly explained that Brant used a zone and the fast break, Templeton played possession and used a weave and block attack, and Southeastern, seeded fourth in the tournament, was small but extremely fast and well conditioned.

"We won't worry about the number-two team, College of the West, right now," he said in conclusion. "We've seen them on TV and we'll see them again Wednesday night."

That evening Chip spent an hour at the New China Tea House with Pete and Jimmy before returning to the hotel to study his scouting notes. He was still studying when Jimmy and Tommy paid him a surprise visit. "We just finished," Jimmy said. "What a week!"

"What a business!" Tommy said proudly. "We've taken in more money in the last four days than we used to take in during a whole month! Pop is going to get a pleasant surprise!"

"We'll see," Jimmy added, his voice a mixture of anxiety and hope. "Anyway, this time tomorrow we'll know."

HAUE A FRIEND, BE A FRIEND

Every team in the tournament had arrived by Monday morning, and all except Southwestern showed up for their lunches and dinners at the New China Tea House. The champions were housed at the Green Mountain Resort, a few miles out of the city.

Coach Corrigan called for another skull practice in the morning, and as soon as it was over, Chip and Speed headed for the restaurant for lunch. "It's now or never," Chip said hopefully.

"Everything's going to be all right," Speed assured him.

The New China Tea House was buzzing! If the ring of customers around the cash register was any indication of his eldest son's business acumen, Li Lu Chung would have to capitulate and support Jimmy's bid for basketball honors and a college education.

Jimmy and Tommy were both scared. Chip could see worry in their eyes and in the furtive glances they kept shooting toward the door. Tommy was hovering by a window overlooking the street and was the first to see his father. He rushed back to the kitchen where Chip was setting up trays for Jimmy and Pete. "Here he comes! Heaven help us!"

Chip followed Jimmy and Tommy out of the kitchen and sat down beside Soapy at the State table. He recognized Mr. Li Lu Chung as soon as he entered the door. The resemblance between the father and his two sons was remarkable.

Li Lu Chung's shoulders were broad and his posture was almost poker-stiff. His straight back made him appear taller than Jimmy or Tommy. He was dressed in a dark suit and tie. His face was broad with high, arched eyebrows, and his thin lips were pinched tightly together. It was easy to tell that this pale-faced man was still ill.

He paused in the door, and Chip thought he saw a quick intake of breath as Li Lu Chung surveyed the busy scene. Then Jimmy and Tommy reached their father's side and bowed from the waist.

Chip could not hear what was being said, but there was no change in Mr. Chung's expression. He bowed and said something, then walked slowly toward the office. Chip noted that the keen dark eyes focused straight ahead, but he was sure Mr. Chung made mental notes of every face and every detail in the room, cataloguing it all for future reference.

Jimmy and Tommy followed their father, looking almost as serious. Tommy brought up the rear, and as he passed Chip, he paused. "He's pleased," he whispered joyfully.

"Then get it over with," Soapy whispered hoarsely.

"You don't know my father," Tommy retorted quickly. "He spends much time in careful thought before making a decision." He hesitated. "If I can only get him to look at the receipts."

It was a long wait. Chip, Speed, and Soapy had been served their lunches, but even Soapy was too anxious to eat much. Soapy sat facing the office door and kept up a rapid-fire flow of words. "Well, come on! What're they doing? Bet they're counting the money! Wish I could be in there. I'd straighten this thing out just like that."

It seemed like an hour, but it was little more than ten minutes later when Jimmy appeared. Alone!

No one had to ask how things had gone. Jimmy's long face told the story. He dropped down heavily in the chair beside Chip and ran his fingers nervously through his hair. Then his head drooped to his chest, and he slumped forward.

"What happened?" Soapy demanded.

Jimmy sighed deeply. "Well, I told him the whole story," he said despondently. "And you know what he said? He said it was a trick, that I was thinking only about basketball and not about my responsibilities as the eldest son. He said my place was here. Ironically, even more so now since I've so successfully demonstrated my ability to manage the business."

"Oh, man!" Soapy managed, moaning deeply.

"How about Tommy?" Chip asked. "Didn't you tell him Tommy could take charge?"

Jimmy nodded. "Sure, Chip. But he wouldn't listen. He said it was my responsibility, not Tommy's."

"Well, I guess that's that," Soapy said. His voice was uncharacteristically tired, and all of his spirit and drive were gone.

"I really thought it would work," Jimmy said, rising slowly to his feet. "And I'm terribly sorry, after you have all worked so hard. I . . . I guess that's about all I can say."

He walked with Chip, Speed, and Soapy as they prepared to leave and paused just outside on the sidewalk.

"How about coming to the game tonight?" Chip asked gently. "We're playing the second game."

"Thanks, Chip," Jimmy said in a low voice. "I'd better . . . Oh, there's my grandfather! I wonder what brings him down here. He seldom leaves the house. Come on. I want you to meet him."

"Your grandfather?"

"Sure. He's a wonderful man."

Chip grabbed Jimmy by the arm. "You mean he's your father's dad?"

"Sure! Come meet him."

Chang Lu Chung was tall and stood very straight and very thin. He had a small face and wore a brown, pointed mustache and a short, old-fashioned Vandyke beard. But it was his eyes that attracted Chip. The alert, dark eyes twinkled at their approach.

Jimmy bowed low and murmured, "Most honorable grandfather."

Chang Lu Chung acknowledged Jimmy's presence with a short bow and glanced at Chip. Chip bowed self-consciously. "Most respected grandfather," Jimmy continued, "this is my beloved friend, Chip Hilton. And these other gentlemen are friends of Chip's: Soapy Smith and Speed Morris."

Chang Lu Chung bowed to each and extended a long, thin hand in greeting. "Pleased to meet friends of my young grandson," he said in a low, pleasant voice.

"I hope my grandson has been most gracious in his reception of his friends, and it is my most humble desire to request a visit to our house when most convenient."

Chip and his friends acknowledged the greeting. Then, with a sympathetic glance at Jimmy, they took their departure.

Chip could hardly contain his excitement. "I've got it!" he said excitedly, as soon as they were out of hearing. "Jimmy's grandfather! I forgot about Jimmy's grandfather! Jimmy's got a grandfather!"

Soapy gave Chip a strange, sideways glance. "Yeah, Chip, we know. Most people do."

"You don't get it. Listen! You know those books I've been reading? Well, the whole of China's old civilization was woven out of the family relationships of father and son, older brother and younger brother. The family is the big thing, and the descent of influence and power in the family stems from the eldest down, no matter how old another member of the family is. Get it?"

Soapy was confused. "No, I don't."

Chip explained patiently. "The eldest son in this case

is Jimmy's father, and the patriarchal father of the whole Chung family is Jimmy's grandfather. Get it now?"

Soapy had got it! "Sure!" he said excitedly. "I get it! The grandfather, the old guy with the beard, is the boss. We've been working on the wrong guy!"

"Right!" Chip said. "Jimmy told me one day that his father had never shown him any affection and always treated him like a man. Well, you just heard him say what a swell person his grandfather was and how he was always making a fuss over him. We learned about that in Chinese history. Anyway, the grandfather can lavish affection on the grandson that he can't show for his own son. That explains the attitude of Jimmy's father."

Soapy nodded. "Right! Now what?"

"We've got to get to the grandfather. Jimmy's father has to do exactly what the grandfather says. Come on! I've got to think this out."

"It sure doesn't seem fair for Jimmy to have to go through all that medieval stuff at home and then try to be like us at school," Soapy said.

"It may not be fair, Soapy, but it's a reality of his life. And it's not medieval stuff to them. We couldn't change that and we wouldn't want to. It's just as real and important to them as our traditions are to us. Right now, our big problem is going to be making contact with Jimmy's grandfather."

"How about asking him to the game?" Speed suggested.

"It's got to be stronger than an invitation," Chip said thoughtfully. "Now if it was some sort of an obligation . . . . You see, the Chinese feel that a debt of one member of the family is a debt of all. That's it! I'll get Jimmy to appeal to his grandfather from the point of view of a debt."

"You mean in terms of what we've done for the restaurant?" Soapy asked.

"Right! I'll call Jimmy from the hotel and get him to put it up to his grandfather that way. You sit with him at the game, OK?"

Soapy nodded emphatically. "Sure! I like that old gentleman."

"You know something, Chip," Speed said tentatively, "we've been putting a lot of thought and work into getting Jimmy back on the team. What if we lose before we get him back?"

"We won't," Chip said grimly. "But if we do, isn't the real objective an education for Jimmy? Isn't the big thing getting Jimmy back in school?"

CHAPTER 18

Beyond the Stars to Reality

CHIP CALLED Jimmy at the New China Tea House as soon as he reached the hotel. "Hello! Jimmy? . . . Chip! Do you think you can get your grandfather to go to the game tonight? Soapy has tickets and can pick him up."

Jimmy was downhearted, and it took a lot of talking and urging before he would agree to talk to his grandfather. Before Jimmy would yield, Chip had to make some pointed references to what Jimmy's friends had done to help him with the New China Tea House.

"All right, Chip," he said at last. "I'll call you right back."

Ten minutes later, Jimmy called back with good news. "All set, Chip. My grandfather will be happy to attend the game."

The two friends agreed that Soapy would pick Mr. Chang Lu Chung up at nine o'clock at the restaurant and accompany him to the game.

"It's up to you now, Soapy," Chip said happily as he

cradled the phone. "Flip on the TV, will you? The first game is about to begin."

A crowd of fifteen thousand fans watched the opening game of the tournament that afternoon. It was a close, tense contest, but Deacon passed Midwestern at the buzzer and won, 73-71. In the second game, Templeton took the lead over Brant early in the first quarter and held on all the way to win 89-72.

"That narrows the field," Soapy said, standing up and stretching.

"I hope we can cut it down a little more!"

"You will! Guess I'd better get back to the restaurant."

Chip passed up the pregame meal and continued to rest. He had always shared Henry Rockwell's belief that the food an athlete ate just before a contest did nothing but slow him down. And when he came out of the elevator at eight o'clock, he felt ready to play the game of his life. The lobby was crowded with fans and friends who had disdained the Kingwood-Wilson University game to escort their team to its game.

In the State University locker room, Murph Kelly worked steadily, taping ankles quickly and efficiently. Word of the Kingwood-Wilson University game filtered in by way of the State manager, Andre Gilbert, who was manning the State locker room door. It was a close fight but Wilson pulled it off, 86-85. The score brought a smile to Chip's lips, and he was happy for Greg and his teammates.

The huge Wilson Arena was jammed with fans when State trotted out on the floor. Chip took his turn in the warm-up and then located his mom, the Morrises, and the Smiths in the third row. Below them, Soapy and Chang Lu Chung were seated directly behind the State bench. Soapy caught Chip's eye and shook his fist over his head in a gesture of support. Chip could tell by the expression on Chang Lu Chung's face that he was amazed. He could see Soapy explaining the game. Gradually, Chang Lu Chung's face relaxed with keen enjoyment as he entered into the enthusiasm of the event. Then he saw the old gentleman lean over and poke a long finger in Soapy's chest. Soapy was having a great time just as he had expected! Chang Lu Chung was quick-witted, an apt sports student, and good fun.

"My grandson would play here too?"

"Sure," Soapy said. "He and Chip are teammates."

"Teammates are important to one another?"

"Yes, they are, Mr. Chung. It's something like the closeness of a family. One for all and all for one. They're important to one another and to their school. Teammates are like brothers."

Chang Lu Chung nodded. "I see. And my grandson is a good player?"

"He sure is! Everyone thinks State could win the championship if he could play." Soapy looked hopefully at his guest, but there was no indication that his words had any effect on Chang Lu Chung. He was watching the game and concentrating on Chip.

Dane was a slow-moving team, and the game was a terrific letdown after the action-packed preliminary. Coach Corrigan started cocaptains Barkley and Thornhill, Bill King, Bradley Gowdy, and Chip.

Early in the game, it became evident that King was in for a big night. His opponent was inches shorter and couldn't stop Bill's shots. But the Statesmen had difficulty in keeping up with Dane, even with King and Chip scoring freely. And once again it was evident that State was just an average ball club, despite the individual brilliance of Chip Hilton. The game was close all the way, but the shooting finesse of Chip Hilton and Bill King made the difference. State won, 73-70.

After the game, Coach Corrigan took the team to the New China Tea House for a late dinner. Jimmy was happy that State had won, but Chip could sense his friend's inner feeling of despair. Li Lu Chung was cool and concerned only with the welfare of the customers. But Chang Lu Chung enthusiastically recounted the events of the night to Jimmy and Tommy.

"It's working," Chip said, nudging Soapy. "Mr. Chang Lu Chung is interested. How did you do it?"

"Easy! I just told him about you and Jimmy. So far so good, but we'd better hurry up! The tournament will be over! What's the next step?"

"We'll wait for one more game. Jimmy said it was folly to rush him. He's our last hope."

"You can say that again. Jimmy's father is cold. I don't think Chang Lu Chung can do anything with him either."

"Then I've been learning a lot of nonsense in my Chinese history class. Chang Lu Chung is the head of the family and will be as long as he lives. Li Lu Chung is the eldest son, and that means Chang Lu Chung is the boss."

"OK, Chip. I believe you. Only you guys better beat Southeastern, or Jimmy will *never* get to come back to school."

The New China Tea House was jammed all day on Tuesday, and all of the Chungs seemed happy with the rejuvenation of the restaurant. And that night when State lined up to face Southeastern, Soapy and Chang Lu Chung were again seated behind the State bench.

Southeastern was fast and liked to run. State couldn't keep up. Chip played the entire first half but was limping badly as the team headed to the locker room. Southeastern led, 48-44.

During the intermission, Murph Kelly worked exclusively on Chip's bad knee, and just before the Statesmen returned to the court, Murph held a short conference with Coach Corrigan. "Better give him a rest, Coach."

Corrigan was disappointed; Chip had scored twenty-seven of State's forty-four points.

But in the last ten minutes, the time when games are won or lost, Coach Corrigan put Chip back in and kept him in the full ten minutes. And it was a good thing he did, because it was Chip's sixteen points and last-second jumper that won the game for State, 91-90. Chip limped all the way, and his points were all outside shots, but State had won.

After the game, when Chip and his happy teammates were in the State locker room, the announcer gave a fast summary of the game. But the fans were so impressed by Chip's forty-three points in thirty minutes of play that their applause drowned out the rest of the State statistics.

Much as Chip would have liked to watch the Southwestern-Deacon game, Murph Kelly prevailed, sending him back to the hotel to rest his knee. So Chip did not see the champions completely demoralize Deacon and win easily with a score of 101 to 54.

Back at Wilson Arena, Soapy further amazed Chang Lu Chung by filling a notebook with circles and dots and dashes. "Scouting notes," he explained. "Scouting notes on the champions, Southwestern. We're going to beat them in the finals!"

Chang Lu Chung pursed his lips and eyed Soapy doubtfully. "The champions appear exceedingly superior. Friend Chip and his teammates have a most difficult assignment."

TOURNAMENT CRISIS

A man seated next to Chang Lu Chung had been listening to the conversation. Now he ventured an opinion. "*Impossible* assignment is more like it."

"Oh, yeah!" Soapy said quickly. "Wait and see."

"I believe you told me that once before," the stranger remarked. "At the New China Tea House. Well, I'm still waiting."

"And we're still winning!" Soapy retorted. Then recognition dawned in Soapy's eyes. "Hey, aren't you a scout?"

The stranger smiled. "I hope so. At least, I'd better be. I'm the Templeton coach, Bill George."

"Hi, Coach George, I'm Soapy Smith and this gentleman is Mr. Chang Lu Chung. Well, you musta been scouting State."

"Right again."

"But why aren't you scouting Southwestern?"

"Well, I know them pretty well. Enough to know no team in this tournament is going to beat them. You're stargazing, Soapy Smith."

"We'll beat 'em!" Soapy insisted. "We've got to beat 'em! We've got some vital reasons."

Coach George nodded. "I know what you mean. You and a lot of other teams," he said dryly. "But you've got a couple of other teams to worry about first."

"You mean your own team, Templeton?"

"Right! College of the West too."

Chang Lu Chung entered the conversation. "Stargazing is most restful to the soul, Coach George," he said blandly. "But a wise man looks beyond the stars to reality. Our young friend is an exceedingly wise gentleman."

"That's right," Soapy agreed proudly. "Ahem! Well, hope you whip College of the West. I'll be pulling for you tomorrow night, but you'll be pulling for State come New Year's Eve!"

Coach George extended his hand. "I root for every team that plays against Southwestern, Soapy. If Templeton isn't playing Southwestern Friday night for the championship, I sincerely hope it will be State. Good night to both of you and good luck."

Chip didn't lack for company after the game that night. Soapy took Chang Lu Chung back to the restaurant and returned to the hotel with Speed, Murph Kelly, Henry Rockwell, and Coach Corrigan. And they brought a snack from Jimmy and Tommy and Pete Thorpe. While Chip ate, they talked about the game, and the conversation shifted to Southwestern and the possibility of Jimmy being able to play.

Soapy was happy and optimistic. "Two to go!" he gloated. "I can just see that big championship crystal basketball right now, sitting on the counter back at Grayson's! Surely State could loan it to us for a few days!"

Coach Corrigan smiled, but he, too, was looking past the stars. "How about Jimmy?"

"That's right," Coach Rockwell added. "How are you making out with his father, Chip?"

"We're not making out. Soapy's trying to win over the grandfather, Mr. Chang Lu Chung, now. He's the patriarchal head of the family, even if he hasn't been working at it, and if Jimmy is going to have a chance to play, it's up to him."

"So that's who you had with you tonight, Soapy," Coach Corrigan said. "I saw you back there behind the bench. How are you making out?"

"Mr. Chang Lu Chung will come around," Soapy answered, his voice expressing more confidence than he felt. "One more game, one more treatment, and he'll give us the restaurant."

"We don't want the restaurant," Rockwell said lightly. "We want to beat Southwestern. If we could be sure of Jimmy for that game, we could be definite with our plans."

Corrigan nodded agreement. "That's right. Even if we had Jimmy for the semifinal game, I wouldn't want to use the press unless we couldn't win without it."

He paused and, after a short silence, continued. "No, our objective is Southwestern and the championship. Just as Rock has so often said, we're taking them one at a time. But, in our hearts, each of us has known ever since the Southwestern game that all our dreams were for another shot at the champions. A chance to square things."

"And," Rockwell added, "if we could count on Jimmy for the championship game, I believe it would give the team enough of a lift to get us by the semifinals Thursday night, whether we have to play Templeton or College of the West."

"Maybe so," Murph Kelly said, rising abruptly to his feet, "but it seems to me you're all overlooking a mighty important element. What if Chip's knee goes bad?"

CHAPTER 19

He Loves the Game

CHANG LU CHUNG surprised both of his grandsons early Wednesday morning when he appeared at the New China Tea House with an armful of newspapers all opened to the sports sections. "My grandsons should be very proud," he said, spreading one of the papers on a table. "Be so good as to note that your distinguished basketball friend is an extremely important gentleman."

A banner headline extended clear across the top of the page.

SOUTHWESTERN AND STATE
GAIN SEMIFINALS
Champions Win Easily and Crush Deacon
State Edges Southeastern in Thriller

Southwestern, the defending champion, seeded number one in the Holiday Invitational, scored an expected easy victory in the nightcap game last night to reach the semifinal round in the top half of the

TOURNAMENT CRISIS

tournament bracket. In the preliminary, State made a dramatic, last-minute surge to defeat Southeastern, 91-90, chiefly through the brilliant play of Chip Hilton. The star sophomore forward scored 43 points, despite being handicapped with a knee injury.

By its victory, Southwestern earned the right to meet the winner of tonight's A & M-Wilson University battle while State will face the victor of the Templeton-College of the West quarterfinal game. Wilson has surprised local fans by standing up through the tough competition of the tourney, and based on the performance of both teams so far in the tournament, Wilson should best the Aggies. The Templeton-College of the West game is a tossup.

State, the Cinderella team of the tournament, may have suffered a disastrous setback last night. Chip Hilton, the Statesmen's scoring sensation, was favoring his right knee late in the game and may be slowed down for the semifinal contest slated for tomorrow night. Despite the injury, Hilton set this year's scoring record, forty-three points, and has averaged thirty-five points in each of the two games in which he has played. His season scoring total in eight games is 253 points in 202 minutes, or 1.25 points per minutes played.

Murph Kelly, State's veteran trainer, is concerned about the condition of Hilton's knee and expects Dr. Mike Terring, State's sports physician, to arrive before the Thursday night game for a consultation. Kelly is especially thankful that Hilton will have nearly two days' rest before the semifinal test.

Southwestern had little trouble with Deacon, and the champions should have no difficulty in sweeping through the coming tests to their third consecutive Invitational crown. College of the West, previously

defeated by Southwestern, is probably best equipped
to make the championship game a contest.

"Rubbish!" Jimmy said. "If Chip's knee is all right,
he'll show them all by himself!"

"My grandson greatly admires his young friend?"

"Yes, revered grandfather. He has done much for me
and for our family. He is a true friend."

Chang Lu Chung nodded. "A distinguished young
man looks beyond the stars," he said cryptically. "I suggest my grandson reads further."

He spread another paper on the table and pointed to
a picture of Chip. "Your young friend appears most certain of the festival's greatest honor. Please note."

CHIP HILTON (STATE) LEADS FIELD
FOR MVP

Chip Hilton, pictured above, racked up forty-
three points last night as he led State to a squeaker
victory over Southeastern's gallant speedsters. It was
a personal victory for the State scoring sensation, and
the brilliant sophomore continues to loom as a shoo-
in for the Most Valuable Player Award. Hilton scored
his forty-three points in exactly thirty minutes of play.

"That's fantastic, Grandpop!" Jimmy said happily.
"Chip deserves all the credit in the world."

"What if he can't play?" Tommy asked, glancing
meaningfully at his older brother.

"State won't win!" Jimmy said gruffly, turning
quickly away.

Chang Lu Chung watched Jimmy walk toward the
kitchen and then turned to Tommy. "My eldest grandson
is extremely fatigued. I suggest he has some relaxation.
Could you manage the restaurant alone tonight?"

TOURNAMENT CRISIS

Tommy nodded and grinned his approval. And that was the reason Soapy was flanked by Chang Lu *and* Jimmy Chung when Templeton defeated College of the West, 52-49, and the hometown heroes, Wilson University, shaded A & M, 87-83.

After the Wilson game, Soapy tried to get Jimmy to join his former teammates at the hotel, but Jimmy insisted he must hurry back to the restaurant. So the three friends walked back to the New China Tea House where Tommy and Pete were waiting.

"Is Jimmy going to play or not?" demanded Pete, who was standing over a hot stove, after Chang Lu Chung and Jimmy had walked into the office.

"We'll know tomorrow," Soapy said.

"If he isn't," Pete blustered, "I'm getting out of here!" He turned to Tommy. "What's the matter with your father?"

Tommy smiled, understanding Pete's frustration only too well. "My father is steeped in old-country customs, Pete," he said gently. "It takes more than just a few days to break down centuries of traditions. Be patient, please."

He turned and walked into the dining room, leaving Pete and Soapy staring at the door.

"It will work out all right, Pete," Soapy said. "I'm going to talk to Mr. Li Lu Chung on my own tomorrow morning, and Chip is just about ready to approach Jimmy's grandfather. Don't worry!"

Murph Kelly said Chip could accompany the team to the New China Tea House for Thursday lunch. As soon as he reached the entrance, Chip knew something was wrong. The tables were crowded, and Soapy was helping Tommy. But Soapy's freckled face was as red as the restaurant's walls used to be, and he avoided the State table as if it didn't exist. Tommy disappeared into the kitchen, and Jimmy immediately came out and sat down beside Chip, his face pale and worried.

"What's wrong with Soapy?" Chip asked.

"Pop," Jimmy whispered. "He's sick again. Early this morning Soapy asked him if I could play in the tournament. Pop blew up and started yelling in Mandarin, and poor Soapy didn't know what he was talking about. Pop was so excited that we had to send for the doctor. He's much better now, and there's no danger; but Soapy is worried and feeling all responsible."

"I'd think so! Are you sure your father is all right? Is there anything I can do?"

"He's OK, Chip. Honest! I wish you would try to explain to Soapy that it wasn't his fault. Pop always has those spells when he gets excited."

Chip followed Jimmy to the kitchen and took Soapy outside to talk. Soapy was all shaky and scared. "I'm sorry, Chip. I've ruined everything."

"No, you haven't. What happened?"

"Well, I wanted to surprise you. I thought Jimmy's father would be so pleased about the restaurant that I could get him to let Jimmy play. So this morning I asked him, and he started yelling at me and then he had some kind of an attack, and now he'll *never* let Jimmy play. And if anything happens to Mr. Chung, it will be my fault."

"Nothing is going to happen to him. Jimmy says he's all right. Now you snap out of it."

It wasn't that easy. Soapy didn't snap out of it, and Chip couldn't do anything to console him. He and Speed went back to the hotel room, but neither of them could relax. They were both too worried about Soapy. Later, Chip called Jimmy and was relieved to find that Li Lu Chung was sitting up at home and was expected back at the restaurant the next day.

"He's more determined than ever that I can't play, Chip. In view of what happened this morning—"

"I know, Jimmy. We won't annoy him anymore. By the way, is your grandfather there?"

"Yes, but—"

"Tell your grandfather I want to talk to him, will you, Jimmy? I'll be there in ten minutes."

"Are you crazy?" Speed demanded when Chip hung up the phone. "You'd better forget about Jimmy Chung and just rest your knee. Haven't you done enough? Anyway, if we don't win tonight, it won't matter whether you talk to Chang Lu Chung or not."

"We'll see," Chip said patiently, pulling on his jacket. "Now where's that clipping about Jimmy?"

"In the desk drawer. You're wasting your time, Chip. Sure, he's been to some practices, but probably not enough to blend in."

Chip found the clipping and tucked it carefully in his pocket. "You're wrong, Speed. Jimmy could blend in with any team, any day and any time, so long as they used the press. He's always in shape, and the press is made for him. We'll never beat Southwestern without him."

"You seem to be forgetting all about Templeton. We'll never beat them without you! And if we don't win tonight, nothing matters."

"That's where you're wrong. *Everything* matters. Besides, we're going to win tonight. Tell Rock I'll be back in time for skull practice. He knows where I'm going and what I'm going to do."

Jimmy and Tommy were waiting and ushered Chip into the office where their grandfather was reading a Chinese newspaper and sipping tea. When they entered the office, Chang Lu Chung bowed solemnly, and Chip bowed in return. The response was automatic and natural.

"Always most happy to see the friend of my grandsons," Chang Lu Chung said pleasantly. "Please be seated."

Jimmy and Tommy disappeared, and Chip launched right in, studying his host's face carefully as he spoke. "Jimmy deserves a chance to finish his education, Mr. Chung. I've been studying Chinese history, and I know how vitally important education and learning are to the Chinese."

Chip hesitated. He scanned Chang Lu Chung's face. There was no change in the inscrutable dark eyes or in the expression on the dignified face.

"You see, Mr. Chung," Chip continued, "Jimmy has told me about his father's home village in China and about all the changes that have taken place there. Jimmy feels that China will never again be the same as it was in the days of his father's youth."

Chang Lu Chung nodded. "That is so, my son," he said gently. "Continue, please."

"Jimmy loves America, Mr. Chung, and he wants to build his future here. His heart is set on getting his college degree and following a career in science as an American. He is proud of his Chinese culture and ancestry, but he *is* an American, sir."

Chip drew the newspaper clipping out of his pocket and placed it in the old gentleman's hand. "Jimmy is a fine student, Mr. Chung, and I know that he didn't send this article home because he didn't want his father to know that he was playing basketball.

"But I think you should know of his accomplishments at State. This piece appeared in the paper this month. Jimmy's professors all feel that he has a great future in the field of science, just as it says right there."

Chip paused again and studied Chang Lu Chung's calm and passive face, but as before, there was no change. He continued slowly. "I hope you will think it over and help Jimmy. You may feel that the guys and I helped Jimmy so he could play on the basketball team. And that's true, but our big reason was to try to get the restaurant established so Jimmy could come back to school. And with Tommy doing such a wonderful job—"

"Jimmy is important to the team?"

"Yes, Mr. Chung, he is. He's a wonderful player and he loves the game with all his heart."

Chang Lu Chung nodded. "Yes, that is not difficult to perceive. However, my eldest grandson has certain family obligations that are far more important at the moment than the game of basketball or his presence at the college." He smiled and extended his hand graciously. "Good afternoon, young friend."

Chip left the office disheartened and low in spirits. He was glad that Jimmy, Soapy, Tommy, and Pete were not in sight. He took a cab back to the hotel and hurried up to the State conference room. Coach Jim Corrigan was chalking "press" notes on the portable strategy board when Chip slipped quietly through the door. Rockwell turned quickly and glanced hopefully at Chip, but the expectant light in his eyes faded when Chip shook his head.

Coach Corrigan paused too. Then he continued. "Coach Rockwell has told you all we know about Templeton, and, as you know, we've been trying to save our special press for Southwestern. But if we have to use it tonight, well, we'll use it! Coach Rockwell and I feel it is the only type of game that can upset Southwestern. And that is the greatest sports desire I have ever experienced—to beat Southwestern. So we'll try to beat Templeton without the press. I think we can do it!"

His words were followed by a tight, tense silence, and the thoughts of most of the players flashed back to the game in which they had been subjected to South-western's humiliating treatment.

"It's too bad Jimmy Chung can't be with us. The method we use in applying the press is entirely new to the game, chiefly because of Jimmy's uncanny inter-cepting ability and skill in dribbling the ball and pulling the opponents out of position. Without Jimmy, it's just another bit of strategy to use in an emergency. Nevertheless, if it's necessary, we'll give it all we've got.

"I know we all feel the same way about South-western. That feeling, the great desire we all possess to get another chance at Southwestern, will help us pull through tonight. A fighting team is hard to beat.

"You're great fighters. I have never coached a more unselfish group. Coach Rockwell and I have been amazed time after time by your close-knit loyalty to one another, once you were welded into a team. That's what team sports are all about. Now one more thing.

"Chip is limping around on a bad leg. Doc Terring will arrive just before game time to give him a final checkup. I hope he gives him a green light, but if he says Chip can't play, well, Chip will have to sit it out."

Dead stillness. Then Corrigan spoke again in the sharp, crisp tones he used in his coaching. "OK. You'll meet in the team room for a light supper and then rest until the game. Any questions?"

There were no questions then or later. Coach Corrigan had said it all. After supper Chip was resting in his room on the bed, looking out the window and gazing far out over the city toward the New China Tea House. He was thinking about Jimmy's fervent hopes and dreams for this night, and all at once Chip's spirits lifted and his heart filled with a great confidence.

CHAPTER 20

Friendship Is Its Own Reward

DR. MIKE TERRING prodded the knee with his sensitive and knowing fingers while he noted the reaction in Chip's eyes. "Sure?" he asked. "Sure this doesn't hurt? Feels pretty tight to me." He glanced doubtfully at Chip again and then turned to Kelly. "All right, Murph," he said brusquely. "He can dress!"

The watchful silence was broken as the players began tugging at jerseys and shoes, and Coach Corrigan and Henry Rockwell moved from player to player with words of encouragement and advice. Minutes later, State was out on the court, fired up with a fierce determination to fight past Templeton and qualify for another chance at Southwestern. There wasn't a doubt in anyone's mind that the champions would take Wilson in the second game.

Chip's knee was tight, and he felt a slight twinge of pain as he trotted through the warm-up drill. But he covered up as best he could, knowing that Templeton's keen-eyed coach, Bill George, was watching every move he made. In the third row, Chip's mom grinned down at her dressed-to-play son as the Morrises caught Speed's eye and the Smiths chatted away.

But behind the State bench, Soapy was sitting alone, an empty seat on each side. It was Chip who clenched a fist this time and shook it encouragingly toward his friend. Then the referee's whistle shrilled, and Chip followed his teammates over in front of the State bench to circle around Coach Corrigan and Coach Rockwell.

There were no last-minute instructions as the State players gripped hands. And it was the same in front of the Templeton bench. Coach George was surrounded by his players, and they were just as quiet as they joined in their team clasp. Then the two teams lined up for the tap, and Chip was gripping the hand of a tall, lean player who smiled as their hands and eyes met and said his name was Bill Johnson. Then the smile vanished, and Johnson appraised Chip warily at close range.

Templeton got the tap, and Chip dropped back on the defense, picking Johnson up as his tall opponent broke for the corner. Johnson broke right out again and then drove hard down the middle, and it took all of Chip's speed to keep up with his opponent's long strides. Johnson had not yet touched the ball. He broke out again and once more cut for the basket at full speed.

Then Chip got it! "He's going to run me all night," he breathed to himself as his knee began to protest the frequent stops and turns and steady running. "Can't let on. Got to put up a good front."

Chip played it smart. He gave no evidence that the pace was too much for him, but he gave Johnson plenty of room. This cut down the distance he had to cover, but it also gave Johnson a chance for a clear shot, and he took it. It was nothing but net, and Templeton was out in front, 2-0. Coach Corrigan was on his feet as soon as the ball swished through the net and called time. Dismayed, Chip saw that J. C. Tucker was moving toward the scorers' table. "I'm all right, Coach," he protested.

"Don't worry, Chip," Corrigan assured him. "Rock and I have something up our sleeves too."

Chip sat it out, groaning inwardly with every Templeton score and grimly watching the big numbers as they steadily mounted on the opponent's side of the scoreboard. At the end of ten minutes, Templeton led, 19-13. Chip hadn't scored a point.

Corrigan gathered the players around him in front of the bench. "Listen, now," he whispered. "Chip is going back in, and we're going to use the switch defense. That will enable Chip to switch off every time Johnson crosses with a teammate. Bill George will have his players keep the middle open to give Johnson room, but he will have to cross someone sooner or later, and Chip can switch off. Try it anyway."

Templeton's Coach George grinned and glanced at Corrigan when State's maneuver was apparent. It was evident he had anticipated the move, because his players immediately reacted to the change in State's defense. When Johnson crossed and Chip switched to another opponent, *that* player immediately cut for the basket at full speed.

As soon as State got the ball again, Coach Corrigan called for another time-out. "We've got it now," he said confidently. "Rock figured it out. Johnson's the only *outside* shooter they have, the only player on their team who can hit from more than twenty feet. So play him tight and float on the rest of them. That goes for Chip and everyone else. Got it?"

It worked! Chip played Johnson tight when he was forced to guard him, and his teammates did the same. But when Chip switched off against one of the other Templeton players, he floated away and rested his knee. The switching helped offensively too. It forced Templeton to change its defensive man-to-man alignment, and Chip broke loose time after time for clear shots. He scored fourteen points in the six minutes he played, but Templeton still led, 41-37, at the buzzer.

Chip played only the first six minutes of the second half and managed to hit for fifteen points, but after ten minutes, Templeton was in the lead by seven points, 61-54. Still, Corrigan did not vary his tactics, and the strategy paid off. Chip, back in the game, got hot, and his teammates fed him the ball every time they got their hands on the precious sphere. Chip hit consistently.

With twenty seconds left to play and Templeton leading 75 to 74, State held the ball for one shot, passing it around in the backcourt and maneuvering so Chip could make the try. With eight seconds left to play and every person in Wilson Arena on his feet, Barkley dribbled to the free-throw line, pivoted, and gave Chip a beautiful handoff as he drove for the basket. Johnson was caught by the pick, but his teammate switched and tried desperately to stop Chip's shot. He was a split second too slow and followed Chip toward the basket. Just as Chip went up for the layup, the frantic player crashed into Chip and knocked him to the floor. The referee's whistle barely beat the buzzer, but there was no doubt about the foul. The official held up two fingers and motioned Chip to the free-throw line.

The pain in Chip's knee was excruciating now, but he gritted his teeth and made it to the line. A streak of fire raced up the side of his leg between the ankle and the thigh, and he bounced the ball several times while he tried to still the trembling muscles of his right leg.

The crowd's silence was deafening; every fan was holding his breath. Chip bounced the ball once again and flipped the ball through the ring to tie the score, 75-75, with one more shot to come. The arena erupted!

Chip managed a pain-riddled step back from the line and looked toward the State bench while the official recovered the ball. It was a flash glance, a desperate search for support from Soapy.

Chip couldn't see Soapy, and the redhead was making no effort to see Chip. Soapy was leaning forward, screened by the standing players, resting his head on his arms draped over the chair in front of him; every fiber of his body tense and straining as he held his breath and prayed for the booming crowd shout of exultation that would signify a successful shot.

In Valley Falls and back in University, thousands of Statesmen fans turned their eyes away from TV screens and waited and hoped and prayed for Gee-Gee Gray's cry of victory.

The officials signaled the crowd for silence as Chip stepped forward to the line and nearly collapsed. His right knee seemed to have lost all its strength, and he stood, swaying slightly from side to side, as he tried to support his weight on the other leg. The crowd gradually silenced, and when it was so still that Chip fancied he could hear the throbbing in his knee, the official handed him the ball.

Chip had to put his weight on his bad leg to hold his balance and nearly cried aloud with the pain. But he controlled the impulse and looked once more for Soapy. Soapy was in plain sight now, standing right on the edge of the floor, both fists doubled and chest held high.

Despite the redhead's emotional stress, he had forced himself out in front to help his pal. His lips were moving soundlessly, but Chip knew what Soapy was saying. And Chip felt he could make it good too!

And he did! The ball went up and out and through the hoop so cleanly that it never touched the rim and barely rippled the cords.

State had beaten Templeton, 76-75, to gain the finals of the Holiday Invitational!

Soapy was out on the floor almost as soon as the ball dropped through the net, and Henry Rockwell and Murph Kelly were right beside him. They made a hand-chair and lifted Chip gently from the floor as he was surrounded by his teammates.

With Coach Corrigan and Mike Terring leading, they fought their way through the fans and the aisle to the State locker room. Andre Gilbert had the door already unlocked and was barring the way to everyone except the coaches and players. The players immediately began to take the locker room apart but straightened up quickly enough when Murph Kelly bellowed for silence. "Chip's hurt, men! Quiet down!"

A quick stillness filled the room, made all the more impressive because of the shouts and din from the hall and the frantic pounding on the door by the newspaper writers who wanted to see Chip Hilton. Twenty minutes later, when Dr. Terring had completed his examination, they sat demoralized by the physician's words:

"Chip is through for the tournament!"

They sat, stunned, for a second. And then, as if it just couldn't be true, they began to ply Dr. Terring with questions.

"You mean he can't play tomorrow against Southwestern?"

"Can't play in the finals?"

"You've got to be wrong, Doc! Just got to be!"

"I wish I was," Terring said sadly.

Chip was stunned too. "Maybe it will be better tomorrow, Doc," he said hopefully.

Terring shook his head. "Not a chance, Chip," he said kindly, placing a hand on Chip's shoulder. "You're a lucky guy, and you're going to stay that way."

Chip slid off the table to the floor. "Look, Doc," he said, sliding his right leg stiffly forward and assaying a step. "I can walk on it all right."

Terring grinned. "OK," he said, nodding, "so you can walk on it! But you're not going to do any running on it! And that's an order."

"Can I suit up for the game tomorrow night?"

"Well, maybe. Murph and I will see what we can work out in the way of a brace while you're taking your shower. Then we'll have a look."

At halftime in the Southwestern-Wilson game, the writers were back. They overwhelmed Andre Gilbert and were firing questions at Dr. Terring, Murph Kelly, and Coach Corrigan when Chip finished his shower.

"You're sure he won't play tomorrow night?"

"Will he be in uniform?"

"How about an operation?"

"If it's not *that* serious, why can't he play?"

"A ligament? Is that worse than cartilage?"

"How can you strain a ligament?"

"I don't get it! He can walk, but he can't run?"

"Oh, you mean it's stiffened up!"

"Seems a shame! Greatest shot I ever saw! Got forty-seven points tonight."

"And he only played twenty-four minutes!"

"Hey, you guys! Second half is about to start."

"Who cares? It's a walkaway! Southwestern is out in front by fifteen points."

It was a walkaway. Southwestern kept pouring it on in the second half to win, 94-61. Coach Jeff Habley never opened the gates of mercy for anyone. When the fans left the arena, they were raving about the prowess of Southwestern and speculating on the kind of performance Chip Hilton, State's star, would have against the champions.

Mr. Chang Lu Chung was beaming happily when he left the house Friday morning. The old gentleman moved slowly and graciously along, attracting some attention because of his stately bearing and dignified carriage. Yes, everything was right with Chang Lu Chung's world. His grandsons, Jimmy and Tommy, had risen with the sun and gone to work; his own son, Li Lu Chung, was once again in good health; the restaurant was a tremendous success, and certainly everything was working out just right for Jimmy's basketball friends . . . or so Chang Lu Chung thought.

He purchased a morning paper at the corner and tucked it under his arm, keeping himself purposefully in suspense about the outcome of the previous night's game. Not that he doubted the results. Hadn't he burned many candles on behalf of Jimmy's basketball friends?

The old gentleman loved his grandsons deeply and lavished the affection upon them that he could not bestow on Li Lu Chung. And he knew their moods as well as his own. The two boys were waiting for him at the New China Tea House and bowed a morning greeting. Chang's keen eyes immediately detected the gloom in their spirits.

"Are my grandsons distressed?"

Jimmy bowed again. "Grandfather has not read the morning paper?"

"I will do so now." He proceeded to the office and opened the paper to the sports page. There he read the full account of the game and all about Chip's injury and the terrific blow it was to State's chances against Southwestern. A few minutes later he left the restaurant without a word to his grandsons. At the corner, Chang Lu Chung hailed a cab and headed toward the center of the city.

The lobby of the Wilsonian Inn was filled with basketball fans, players, and coaches, and Chang Lu Chung was known by sight to some of them. These spoke; others commented upon his tall, trim figure.

Soapy, Speed, Kirk Barkley, and Greg Moran were with Chip when Chang Lu Chung knocked on the door of Chip's hotel room. The elderly gentleman bowed to Soapy, entered the room, and crossed quickly to the chair in which Chip was sitting. He bowed to Chip, motioning him to remain seated, and offered Chip his hand. "My young friend has experienced ill fortune. The Chung family is extremely concerned and hopes for a quick recovery. Are you hurt badly?"

Chip smiled. "The injury itself isn't too serious, Mr. Lu Chung. I can move around as long as I don't run."

"So you cannot play in the important game tonight?"

"No, Mr. Lu Chung. I guess I'll be out of basketball for awhile."

Chang Lu Chung nodded slowly and studied the support strapped around Chip's knee. "Will you be at the game?"

"Yes, Mr. Lu Chung, I'll be there all right. I'll be in uniform, too, even though I can't play."

FRIENDSHIP IS ITS OWN REWARD

"I'll say he'll be there," Soapy said grimly. "We'll all be there, even if we have to crawl!"

"This is an important matter for all of you," Chang Lu Chung said, eyeing each of the boys, "this basketball championship."

"Yes, it is, Mr. Lu Chung," Chip said softly. "I wanted to play in this game more than any other in my life. It's important to the school and the coaches, but it's especially important to my friends."

Chang Lu Chung nodded. "I understand. Friendship means much to you. That is a fine thing. Friendship and the team spirit young Soapy was telling me about. They are extremely important.

"Well, my friend, I wish you a speedy recovery. And I agree with you that friendship is priceless and is its own reward." He bowed and walked to the door, pausing with his hand on the knob. "Your friend Soapy also advised me of an axiom that I find most familiar. It goes something like: 'One for all and all for one.'"

He paused once more and then continued with feeling. "In Old China, a debt of one member of the family is a debt of all members of the family. Good afternoon, my friends."

CHAPTER 21

One More Shot

KIRK BARKLEY was bewildered. He waited until the door closed and then turned to Chip. "What was *that* all about? What does he mean, 'Friendship is its own reward'?"

"He means we ought to be happy because the New China Tea House is a big success!" Speed said bitterly. "Sure! Everything is just great! Chip, Soapy, Pete Thorpe, Greg Moran, and the rest of us work our heads off so we can get Jimmy back on the team, and he gives us a lot of double talk! Friendship! Hah!"

"Take it easy, Speed," Chip remonstrated. "I think it was nice of him to come."

"Right!" Soapy agreed. "He's a wonderful man."

"Well, if he's so wonderful," Speed retorted, "why doesn't he tell Jimmy's father off? You said yourself, Chip, that he was the real boss of the family, the patriarchal father or whatever you call it. He sure doesn't act like it."

ONE MORE SHOT

Meanwhile, Chang Lu Chung had stopped in the lobby of the hotel to pick up an afternoon paper, which he read in the taxi on the way back to the New China Tea House. He was especially thoughtful as he studied Chip's picture and read the article centered directly in the middle of the first page of the sports section.

FAMOUS STATE STAR SIDELINED
Southwestern Conceded Easy Championship
Victory Tonight

Chip Hilton, leading in Holiday Invitational Tournament scoring, suffered an injury to his knee last night that will force him to watch tonight's championship game between Southwestern and State from the sidelines.

Hilton scored forty-seven points last night and won the thrilling battle after time ran out. With ten seconds left to play and Templeton leading, 75-74, State's Kirk Barkley passed to Hilton in a last-hope try for a score. Hilton took the pass and drove for the basket. Just as he released the ball, he was fouled.

Only a few of the 24,885 fans in huge Wilson Arena realized that the famous star had been injured on the play. Hilton sank the two free throws to make the score State 76, Templeton 75. The win put his team in the final championship game.

Hilton won't be able to compete tonight in the title game. The loss of the brilliant star makes State a hopeless underdog, and most observers feel that Southwestern, the team the experts call the greatest in basketball history, will win in a walkaway and wrap up its third-consecutive Holiday Invitational Tournament title.

TOURNAMENT CRISIS

The victory margin can be measured only by the number of points Coach Jeff Habley feels will be necessary to humiliate his opponents.

Chang Lu Chung thrust the paper aside and tapped the taxi driver on the shoulder. "Please change our destination," he said.

Later that afternoon, when Chip limped into the New China Tea House with Soapy and his teammates for the last meal before the championship game, every table, except the one reserved for State, was filled. Li Lu Chung was standing just inside the entrance, but when he saw Soapy he walked to the other side of the dining room and warily watched his redheaded nemesis from afar.

Jimmy and Tommy and Pete immediately dropped all other business and joined them. "How ya feeling, champ?" Pete asked. "How's the leg?"

"Fine, Pete."

"You sure you can't play?"

"Absolutely. Doc Terring's orders. If we only had Jimmy . . ."

Pete glowered across the dining room at Li Lu Chung. "For two cents—" he began.

"I know," Chip said hastily. "Forget it!"

It was an awkward meal. Pete sat in a chair beside Chip, and Jimmy and Tommy seemed to have forgotten all about the other customers. Coach Corrigan made the break, handing Jimmy a fistful of tickets. "Here's some tickets. They're for right behind our bench. Try to make it. You, too, Pete and Tommy. Well, wish us luck."

It was impossible to get near the Wilson Arena that night. Fans jammed the streets, alleys, and sidewalks. Cars lined every street and alley, some even perched on people's lawns, and the arena parking lot had been filled for hours. There was obviously some miscommunication because two overly zealous members of campus security stopped the State bus and would not allow it to turn onto Campus Drive, the entrance to the arena. The team would have to alight there and go the rest of the way on foot. Coach Corrigan was furious, but his arguing got him nowhere and the clock was ticking. So Chip hobbled along behind his teammates.

The main lobby was filled with a solid block of unyielding humanity that resented every push until the fans recognized the State players. As if by common consent, a path opened for them as well-wishers patted their backs and offered encouragement.

Finally, the team reached the State locker room and began to dress. Chip felt ridiculous putting on a uniform when he couldn't play and mentioned something to Murph about not dressing. Coach Corrigan and his teammates wouldn't stand for it! "We're all in this together," Murph Kelly muttered, checking Chip's knee brace.

"That's right," Coach Corrigan agreed. "And that means you, too, Smith."

Soapy's mouth fell open, and he stared at Corrigan as if he couldn't believe his ears. "Me, Coach? Me?"

"Yes, you! We want you sitting on the bench for good luck. Seriously, Soapy, next to Chip. We all realize that no one has worked harder or done more to help Jimmy and to win this tournament than you. Right, guys?"

The cheer the players gave Soapy then was a far greater reward than the happy-go-lucky redhead ever desired or expected. He flushed and shot a self-conscious glance at Chip. Chip was grinning and cheering with the rest, and Soapy suddenly found it necessary to bend over and pick up some lint or something from the floor. Then, while Murph was finishing taping ankles, Coach Corrigan and Rock followed through with their old practice of moving from one player to the next with encouragement and advice.

Someone banged on the door, and Andre Gilbert opened it an inch and peered out. Then be relayed the message: "We're due on the court for the pregame ceremonies in five minutes, Coach."

A violent banging on the door interrupted him, and Corrigan turned impatiently to Gilbert. "Don't open the door!" he said sharply.

Outside, a babble of voices grew louder and the pressure on the door increased, forcing Gilbert back. Corrigan was thoroughly upset now and gestured to Kelly. "Help him out, Murph. *No one* comes into this locker room!"

"Hold it, Coach!" Soapy cried. "That's Mr. Chung's voice! And Jimmy too!" He rushed to the door and pulled it open. Then he took one look and fell back in amazement. "Mr. Lu Chung!" he gasped.

This was a night of surprises, but no one was prepared for the sight of Chang Lu Chung as he stepped into the room. His tall, erect figure was clad in a stylish, midnight-gray suit. He wore a white shirt with a black striped tie and twirled a cane with his right hand. He smiled at Coach Corrigan and bowed, and for the first time the startled players noticed that his mustache and beard were gone. Crowding in behind him came Li Lu Chung, Tommy Chung, Pete, and Jimmy.

"Jimmy!" Chip cried, forgetting his leg and leaping forward. "You're going to play!"

"Chip speaks correctly," Chang Lu Chung said calmly. "The Chang Lu Chung family much appreciates what our friend Soapy said about 'One for all and all for one,' and it is hoped my grandson's efforts may partly repay his debt to such illustrious friends. A debt of one member of the Chung family is a debt of all."

Jim Corrigan was the first to recover from the shock. He grabbed Kelly by the arm. "Give him a uniform, quick Murph!"

Confusion reigned. Chang Lu Chung and Li Lu Chung were trying to help Jimmy undress, speaking in Mandarin, and doing more to hinder than help him. The rest of the players stared with amused but happy eyes at the mad action.

Then the game buzzer cut through the turmoil, and Corrigan led the players toward the court, shouting over his shoulder. "Hurry up, Murph. We're starting Jimmy in place of Tucker."

Somehow, someway, Murph Kelly got Jimmy dressed. As Soapy was about to leave the room, Murph called him back and handed him a warm-up jacket with a big 50 on the back. "Here," Murph growled, "you're one of us. Put this on."

"It's an omen!" Soapy cried. "Southwestern's after game number 50, and I've got it on my back! That's one number they'll *never* get!"

"Come on!" Kelly growled. "We've got a job to do!"

Out on the court, the pregame ceremonies had been completed and Jimmy had joined in the State warm-up drill. His presence created a stir among the fans and writers, and Coach Corrigan sent Henry Rockwell over to the scorers' table to make sure Jimmy was entered in the scorebook and to explain his presence to the writers.

Jimmy's name had never been removed from the roster, and the fans quickly identified him. Jimmy made his presence known quickly enough, and the program helped. When the two teams lined up for the opening center tap,

TOURNAMENT CRISIS

Southwestern towered over the State players like a college squad over a team of middle schoolers.

Surprisingly, Sky Bollinger got the tap. Bordon took it easy, and State was away, all five players breaking for the basket like runaway horses. Sky took a pass from Bitsy Reardon and scored before Bordon got out of the center circle. But that was just the start. During the next three minutes, Kirk Barkley was the only State player to drop back under the Southwestern basket on defense.

Jimmy Chung, Speed Morris, Bitsy Reardon, and Sky Bollinger met the bewildered champions in the State end of the court three straight times and stole the ball three times for three easy baskets. The four speedsters dashed wildly after the ball, double-teaming opponents when possible, switching when necessary, and playing for an interception on every pass.

The fans rose to their feet en masse when Jimmy stole a pass right out of Reggie "Allnet" Ralk's hands and dribbled all alone under the State basket for another unguarded shot. That made the score State 10, Southwestern 0, and Jeff Habley bellowed for a time-out, his face red with anger.

The crowd noise never slackened during the time-out. State's racehorse tactics were as much a surprise to the fans as they were to the national champions. Jeff Habley was raging in the huddle of players in front of the Southwestern bench, shaking a fist under the noses of his players and yelling at the top of his voice.

It helped the champions a little, but it was obvious Southwestern had been caught asleep. Then the Southwestern players made a bad mistake, the mistake Chip had figured they might make. They tried to outrun State. The effort backfired; the game became a runaway scoring match, with all science and all thoughts of defense flying out the window. Despite Jeff Habley's berating shouts and mad bellowing, he could not control his players.

Jimmy was sensational! He was all over the court, making unbelievable interceptions, setting up scoring plays for his teammates, and, in the process, scoring thirty-seven points himself. State led, 62-53 at the half, and the crowd was still cheering Jimmy and his teammates minutes after they left the court.

Jimmy put his arm around Chip, and they walked back to the locker room together with Soapy leading the way and elbowing a path through the fans who were trying to get a good look at Jimmy and Chip.

Inside, Coach Corrigan, Coach Rockwell, and Murph Kelly were working furiously over the players, almost as excited as the fans who thronged the hall outside the door. Corrigan didn't say very much when it was time to go back out on the floor. There wasn't much he could say. But he did warn his players that Southwestern was a great ball club. He also reminded them of the great spurt the champions had taken in the second half of the "treatment game."

"Only twenty minutes to go, team! Don't back down an inch! How are you feeling, Jimmy? Good! All right, same team! No changes and no letdown! Now, go get 'em!"

The Statesmen filed out through the crowd, and as they passed the Southwestern locker room they could hear Coach Jeff Habley yelling at the top of his voice. The fans called encouragement and tried to get as close to the Cinderella team as possible.

"That's Hilton! Too bad he couldn't play tonight!"

"Must have been keeping this Chung guy hidden!"

"This is gonna be the biggest upset in the history of basketball!"

"It's not over yet. Southwestern's a second-half ball club."

"Sure didn't look like champions the first half!"

"Be different now. Habley will fire 'em up!"

Southwestern still hadn't returned from the locker room as the second half was about to begin. Coach Corrigan glanced at the game clock and sent the State players out on the court to line up. They stood there until the referee waved them back to their bench and sent the umpire for Southwestern. But the umpire came right back, shaking his head, and said something to the referee. Then Coach Corrigan sent State back out on the court, and this time the referee went to the Southwestern locker room himself. And when the champions finally did appear, the referee penalized them with a technical foul, and the alternating possession arrow now pointed to State.

Then Coach Habley really put on an act in front of his bench, yelling at the officials at the top of his voice. And he was still yelling when Kirk Barkley dropped the ball through the hoop to give State a twelve-point lead, 67-55.

Coach Habley's sideline actions seemed to set the pattern for the Southwestern players, who began to use their rough stuff. Munn sent Jimmy sprawling with a shove. The act went undetected, and Chip watched Jimmy anxiously, fearing he might fall into the trap and lose his head. But Jimmy glanced over at Chip and winked. Chip breathed a sigh of relief. Jimmy knew the score.

It was a rough, tough, knock-'em-down, dragout game, and Southwestern slowly but surely closed the gap. The officials didn't let the game get out of hand; they kept calling the fouls and these kept State in the game. With just under ten minutes left to play, State led 87-85.

From that moment on, Coach Jeff Habley was on his feet with every call, protesting and yelling at the officials. These tactics drew another technical foul. But the champions were aroused now and played desperately, and their weight, height, and endurance began to tell. They caught up, tied the score, and then went out in front by five points, 103-98, with four minutes left to play.

Then, just when State's cause seemed hopeless, Jimmy stole the ball twice in a row while Southwestern was attempting a freeze; he scored both times. That brought the Statesmen back into contention, only a point behind, with the score Southwestern 103, State 102. Jeff Habley called for a time-out.

Jimmy was out on his feet, and Coach Corrigan used his last time-out as soon as the Southwestern time-out ended. "That's it, men," he said. "We've used our last one, so for goodness sake, don't ask for another one."

There were two minutes and two seconds left to play when Ralk and Munn brought the ball upcourt. All the drive had gone out of Sky Bollinger and Kirk Barkley and Speed Morris. The press was impossible. Only Jimmy and Bitsy still possessed the reserve strength to keep pressing, and it was Jimmy who dove for the ball and forced Munn to make a bad pass. The ball was just out of Ralk's reach, but his fingers got enough of the ball to deflect it out of bounds in front of the Southwestern bench.

Then Jeff Habley made a disastrous mistake. Almost as if by instinct, without seemingly giving it a thought, the excited man sprang to his feet and pushed Jimmy roughly away from the ball! And as Jimmy recovered and leaped for the ball, Habley kicked it!

Every fan in Wilson Arena gasped at the man's audacity and stupidity. The referee was so surprised—

shocked, actually—that he was late in blowing his whistle. But he called the technical foul, pointed to Habley, and walked briskly to the State free-throw line. This was Habley's third technical foul, and he was ejected from the game!

Habley shouted for another time-out, and when his players gathered in front of the bench, he ignored them completely and began yelling at the officials. While the official explained that State would shoot two shots and then take the ball out of bounds, Habley slumped in his chair. Politely, the official reminded the Southwestern coach he was to leave the bench area and go to his locker room for the remainder of the game. Coach Corrigan took advantage of the time-out to talk to his team. "You shoot them, Barkley," he said.

"I can't, Coach. I'm all used up!"

Corrigan glanced around the circle of tired, drawn faces and made a sudden decision. "Chip!" he called. "Quick! Report for Barkley! Shoot the free throw!"

Before Chip could catch his breath, Henry Rockwell lifted him to his feet. "You've got to do it, Chip. The team needs you now. Make the shot, Chip, and then take the ball out of bounds. Pass it in and stay out of the play. Got it? And, Chip, a little higher and a little harder."

A tremendous cheer greeted Chip as he stripped off his warm-up jacket and limped to the scorers' table with the knee brace securely in place. And it grew in volume as he made it to the free-throw line and took the ball. He glanced at the scoreboard: Southwestern 103, State 102.

Chip felt it was all a dream. He moved his feet into position, making sure that the toes of his basketball shoes did not infringe upon the free-throw line, and glanced at the basket. Then he bounced the ball and concentrated on the spot on the rim. The tension of the crowd seemed to move in and envelop him like the fog of a dark, misty night.

And as Chip bounced the ball, it seemed he could hear the Rock saying, "When you're tired and tight and jittery, Chip, shoot a little higher and a little harder and make sure you follow through with your hands."

The crowd felt the suspense now, and the shouts and cheers became a steady roar. The official stepped in front of Chip and held up his hands for silence. It was to no avail. No one could have silenced the roar of that crowd. He waited several seconds and then shrugged his shoulders and stepped back out of the lane. "Take your time, son," he said. "I can't do anything with them."

Chip bounced the ball twice, took a deep breath, and aimed. Then he let it go, a little higher and a little harder and with a little more follow-through. The ball went spinning up and out and down through the hoop and swished through the cords to tie the score!

The big numbers on the scoreboard blinked hard and fast and off and on, and there it was: Southwestern 103, State 103.

Pandemonium! Thundering turmoil! A deafening and tumultuous roar mixed with relief, frustration, anguish, and joy. Then it dwindled as the drama on the floor brought realization that the issue was still in doubt. There was one more shot.

CHAPTER 22

We Learn from the Young

GEE-GEE GRAY was beside himself with excitement and tension up in the broadcasting booth. "The second shot is also good! It's State's ball out of bounds now. Hilton is going to pass it in. The ball is dead until it touches a player on the court, you know—

"Hilton fakes to Morris and throws the ball to Bollinger—the big center leaps high in the air—oh, no! Bollinger fumbled Hilton's pass, fans. Bordon has the ball now. He passes it over to Ralk, and the great all-American passes it over to Lloyd and drives toward the basket. Hilton is limping down the court—there's no way he can keep up with Ralk.

"Jim Lloyd and Joe Munn are bringing the ball upcourt—Munn glances at the shot clock to make sure there is plenty of time. Every fan in this colossal arena—all twenty-five thousand of them—shifts his eyes to follow Munn's glance.

"The fans have really been attuned to the action here

tonight ever since State unveiled its bewildering press attack. But it has worn them out. Through all the fury of this great game, every person in this building has avidly followed the brilliant play of these two great teams. Most of the spectators here can hardly believe what they are seeing.

"Under ten seconds on the shot clock. Over to Lloyd, back to Munn, in to Bordon! Two-Ton shoots!

"He missed! That was a rushed shot by Bordon. But he managed to rebound his own shot, and now Southwestern has a fresh shot clock and they're down by one point.

"Bordon passes out to Ralk. The famous star pivots away from Hilton and holds the ball while he checks the time.

"Just over a minute and twenty seconds to go! The players and coaches are standing at their benches. You can see the tension and pressure etched in their faces. Fans, this is basketball at its most intense!

"The Southwestern players are chanting: 'Hold that ball! Hold that ball!' And right across the scorers' table from them, almost shoulder to shoulder, the State players are screaming: 'Get that ball! Get that ball!'

"Coach Jeff Habley is sure missing a great game. Sure glad I'm not his assistant taking over in this spot!"

Through the roar, Chip could hear the assistant coach shouting, "Ralk! Watch out! You hear me, Ralk? Give the ball to Perkins! Over to Munn now! You hear me? Pass and cut away. *Away* from the ball!"

Chip glanced at the clock. Sixty seconds left in the game and almost five on the shot clock for Southwestern . . . If he could only call a time-out. He gave Ralk a little more room, backed up, and waited with bated breath. And the same words were running through his thoughts time after time: "If Ralk cuts now, I'm lost."

TOURNAMENT CRISIS

Gee-Gee Gray was leaning over the side of the broad-casting box, every fiber of his being tingling with the excitement of the tense climax. "Joe Munn shoots from the side—this one clangs against the rim—the shot clock reset as the ball bounded right into Perkins's hands.

"State should have gotten that rebound, but they're worn out and trying to hold on to the slimmest of margins—one point. Southwestern has gone cold; I don't know why they aren't taking advantage of their mismatch with Hilton on the floor yet not mobile. Seems like each one of them wants to make the last shot, the winning shot.

"Perkins fakes a pass to Munn in the corner and fires the ball to Ralk. Ralk catches the ball and pivots away from Hilton. He holds the ball at arm's length while he studies the clock. It is a magnificent display of confidence. That's why they've won forty-nine in a row!"

Down on the sideline, in front of the Southwestern bench, the bewildered assistant was still pleading. "Just takes one shot, Reggie! Hold it! One shot! Hold that ball! Hear me, Reggie? Watch out! Give it to Lloyd!"

From the State bench came heart-rending pleas and shouts.

"Go get that ball!"

"*Do* something! Don't just stand there!"

"You've *got* to *do* something!"

Gray was spelling the story out over his headset to millions of listeners, his quick eyes catching every move on the court.

"Ralk glances tantalizingly over his shoulder at Hilton and jerks the ball back as if threatening to throw it in the injured State star's face—it's just a gesture, of course.

"This could be it fans! Southwestern is set to go with eight seconds on the shot clock and twenty-eight on the game clock. Ralk's ignoring Hilton now—Ralk zips the ball toward Lloyd and cuts for the basket."

On the court, taut and keyed to an almost heart-breaking pitch, Jimmy had been playing decoy against Lloyd. What happened then was so unexpected that most of the fans missed the play entirely.

Jimmy shot forward like a flash of light. The lunge of his body and the desperate thrust of his hand were too fast to be seen. But he hit the ball!

Reggie "Allnet" Ralk had expected a return pass for the go-ahead basket after he cut away from Chip. But, too late, he had seen Jimmy poise for the interception. "No!" he shouted. "No! Watch out!" Then he turned and dashed for the State basket, still shouting, "No! No!"

Twenty-five thousand voices rose in a thundering crescendo to testify to the interception.

Gee-Gee Gray had seen the play, had found himself shouting, his voice vibrant with emotion. "Chung slips—he goes to one knee—now he's up and driving forward! He slaps the ball again—the precious sphere bounces. Jimmy Chung is over it now, and the ball is responding to the deftness of his touch as if it is an appendage.

"Ralk is standing as if paralyzed, fans. He's trying to fight back the realization that Chung has stolen the ball and is on his way toward the State basket. He has taken off after Chung, ignoring Hilton completely.

"Lloyd is ahead of Chung—he's got a ten-foot start over his opponent as he heads diagonally for the basket—Lloyd is fast, and his long legs are edging him ahead of Chung.

"Jimmy Chung swerves away, and I can hear the sigh of the Southwestern rooters clear up here in the broadcasting booth.

TOURNAMENT CRISIS

"Chung is dribbling away from Lloyd now and toward the side of the court. The crowd is quieting a bit.

"Southwestern is back on defense now, and Reggie Ralk has paired up against Jimmy Chung. There's less than twenty seconds to play, State is up by one, and neither team has any time-outs.

"Munn made a move away from Chip Hilton just now, fans, but he moved back when Hilton hobbled toward the open basket. Ralk is on his own again; he simply can't catch his elusive opponent!

"It's no contest, fans! Ralk is discouraged."

Chip was trying to keep Munn out of Jimmy's way and caught only a glimpse of Jimmy's maneuvers. But he heard the giant wave of applause from friend and foe alike and heard it pick up in volume and sweep down and around the court as Jimmy toyed with Ralk and played for time.

Chip checked the time, keeping his eyes focused on the clock. Fifteen seconds . . . fourteen seconds . . .

Jimmy's eyes were fixed on the clock too. He kept up his dribbling: tap-tap, tappity-tap, tap-tap, guiding the precious ball with his supple fingers. The ball bounced this way and that, forward and back, and left and right as if it was the shadow of his hand. And through it all, Jimmy was seemingly oblivious to Ralk, expressing no obvious desire to humiliate his furious opponent.

Chip was counting aloud now: "Nine seconds! Eight! Seven! . . ."

Then Jimmy maneuvered to the right, faked back, and then drove to the right.

And while Chip was counting and hoping and pulling for his friend with all his heart, Jimmy dribbled behind his back and cut in the opposite direction. Ralk made a final, desperate lunge for the ball, but it was a futile gesture.

Jimmy took off from the free-throw line and let the shot go just as the big clock clicked back to 00:00. Chip tried to follow the flight of the ball, but he never saw it drop through the hoop. He heard only the tremendous crowd roar. Then his teammates dashed out on the court just as the buzzer ending the game sounded!

The ball flew straight and sure and never touched the rim; it swished through the cords as if it had eyes, just as the buzzer drilled through the deafening roar.

State had accomplished the impossible. The Statesmen had tumbled mighty Southwestern to its first defeat after forty-nine consecutive victories and had won the Holiday Invitational Tournament: State 106, Southwestern 103.

Hysteria gripped almost everyone in the arena, with the notable exceptions of Chang Lu Chung and Li Lu Chung. They sat immobile, inscrutable, and calm, watching the mad antics of the fans and players as if unable to understand the why or wherefore of the scene. Out on the court, the jubilant State players had lifted Jimmy to their shoulders and were already surrounded by fans. And then they swarmed back and hoisted Soapy with the big 50 on the back of his red-and-blue warm-up jacket to their shoulders. Then they joined the mob on the floor.

Many of the fans were amazed at this development. "Wonder what that's all about?" they cried.

"*He* wasn't in the game!"

"Number 50 isn't even listed in the program!"

Inside the locker room, the triumphant warriors unceremoniously dumped Jimmy and Soapy under the shower and gave Chip and Chang Lu Chung and Li Lu Chung a resounding cheer.

Corrigan and Rockwell made the mistake of rushing

in to join the celebration at that moment, and they, too, ended up under the shower, clothes and all!

There was a great pounding at the door, and the tournament officials and several arena security officers barged into the locker room. "Your team is wanted out on the floor!" the excited director shouted. "They're waiting to give you the prizes. You won the tournament! Or didn't you know?"

"Yes," another added. "And that means pictures and the trophy and tournament watches! C'mon! Can't you hear the crowd? They're waiting for you champs!"

Seconds later, when the soaking wet Holiday Invitational Tournament champions walked out onto Wilson's preciously polished floor, a great cheer greeted them. And it exploded and boomed out into the hall where Chip Hilton, flanked on either side by Chang Lu Chung and Li Lu Chung, was being unnecessarily escorted toward the court.

The fans were subjected to another surprise on this great night of upsets when Chang Lu Chung and Li Lu Chung walked Chip right out before the table where all the prizes rested. The director's voice drilled through the sound system then, announcing that the tournament committee had found it difficult to select one player as the most valuable.

"We have, therefore," the director said, "decided to select two great players from the same team, and they will be awarded identical MVP plaques! Ladies and gentlemen, athletes, coaches, and fans, I give you Chip Hilton and Jimmy Chung!"

The New China Tea House was jammed. Every seat was taken, and every inch of space along the walls was lined with fans and customers and college students. All had joined in the hilarious celebration and were waiting eagerly for Soapy Smith's New Year's Eve party to begin.

In the middle of the main dining room, the State basketball team and other celebrities were ensconced at a long table covered with favors and horns and main dishes and sandwiches and cakes and relishes and salads and cold cuts and fruit and nuts and so many other Chinese and American delicacies that even Pete Thorpe and Tommy Chung couldn't name them all.

And right in the center of the table, the large, luminously beautiful Waterford Crystal basketball was displayed with ribbons leading to all the places at the table of honor.

Chip and Jimmy were seated on each side of Gee-Gee Gray in the seats of honor. Li Lu Chung and Chang Lu Chung were next, and then around the table were Coach Jim Corrigan, Henry Rockwell, Doc Terring, Murph Kelly, Bob Chandler, Greg Moran, Kirk Barkley, Randy Thornhill, Bradley Gowdy, Bill King, Dom Di Santis, Sky Bollinger, Rudy Slater, Speed Morris, J. C. Tucker, Bitsy Reardon, and Andre Gilbert, the manager. Pete and Tommy Chung hovered over the table, worried that some of their guests might feel slighted.

All the players' parents and siblings were seated at tables surrounding the head table. Everyone was celebrating State's marvelous success and looking to the new year ahead.

The din was deafening, but somehow Gee-Gee Gray got the guests to quiet down before the speeches began. Gee-Gee called on Chip and Jimmy and Coach Corrigan and Soapy and Barkley and Thornhill and Murph Kelly and Bob Chandler. Bob got a big hand when he said, "Don't forget, Wilson University won third place!"

Then Gray introduced Li Lu Chung. The proprietor

of the New China Tea House stood with dignity, although he had some difficulty finding the right words. Some of the fans couldn't hear him, but every syllable came through to Chip Hilton.

"In Chinese society, although an elder is revered, sometimes we can learn much from the young." Then Mr. Chung smiling broadly said, "You'll be happy to know, my number-two son, Tommy, is taking over as manager of New China Tea House while my eldest son, Jimmy, pursues both education and basketball with his coaches and teammates at State University."

• • •

STATE UNIVERSITY'S troubles on the court are compounded when Chip Hilton, sensational sophomore scorer, is benched by a knee injury. When State is beaten by their hometown rival, Tech, and a sour sportswriter attacks Chip's integrity, things take a turn for the worse. Just when it seems nothing else could go wrong, Soapy is identified as the prime suspect in a string of convenience store robberies!

Be sure to read *Hardcourt Upset,* a blend of sports action and mystery—another thrilling Chip Hilton Sports series adventure by Coach Clair Bee.

Afterword

TO RANDY AND CINDY FARLEY, a million thanks for the reflective memories in revising the Chip Hilton series! For many of us who have delved into Clair Bee's books, precious memories abound that last a lifetime.

The Chip Hilton series presents life in all aspects of living. Two of my favorite books are *A Pass and a Prayer* and *Hoop Crazy*. Each book detailed human qualities for successful living and also taught us that true champions never quit.

Coach Clair Bee was a man for all seasons. In our lifetime we meet people who stand out from the rest. He epitomized super talents in a myriad field of endeavors and taught all of us to pursue the highest of goals in the grace of perseverance. He imparted in all not to be fearful of failure; that sometimes fears may seem insurmountable, but through persistence and courage we should continue to be successful.

My wife, Rose, and I had the opportunity to work

with Coach Bee at New York Military Academy and Kutsher's Sports Camps while our two sons, Mark and Mel, were campers.

As time passes on, I shall always appreciate the influence and impact that both Coach Bee and the Chip Hilton series have had on my personal and professional life. And I trust the revised Chip Hilton series will prove to be as successful in the new millennium as the original series was in the past.

COACH MARLO M. TERMINI

Your Score Card

I have read: I expect to read:

___   ___   1. **Touchdown Pass:** The first story in the series, introducing you to William "Chip" Hilton and all his friends at Valley Falls High during an exciting football season.

___   ___   2. **Championship Ball:** With a broken ankle and an unquenchable spirit, Chip wins the state basketball championship and an even greater victory over himself.

___   ___   3. **Strike Three!** In the hour of his team's greatest need, Chip Hilton takes to the mound and puts the Big Reds in line for all-state honors.

___   ___   4. **Clutch Hitter!** Chip's summer job at Mansfield Steel Company gives him a chance to play baseball on the famous Steelers team where he uses his head as well as his war club.

___   ___   5. **A Pass and a Prayer:** Chip's last football season is a real challenge as conditions for the Big Reds deteriorate. Somehow he must keep them together for their coach.

___   ___   6. **Hoop Crazy:** When three-point fever spreads to the Valley Falls basketball varsity, Chip Hilton has to do something, and fast!

TOURNAMENT CRISIS

I have   I expect
read: to read:

____   ____   7. **Pitchers' Duel:** Valley Falls participates in the state baseball tournament, and Chip Hilton pitches in a nineteen-inning struggle fans will long remember. The Big Reds year-end banquet isn't to be missed!

____   ____   8. **Dugout Jinx:** Chip is graduated and has one more high school game before beginning a summer internship with a minor-league team during its battle for the league pennant.

____   ____   9. **Freshman Quarterback:** Early autumn finds Chip Hilton and four of his Valley Falls friends at Camp Sundown, the temporary site of State University's freshman and varsity football teams. Join them in Jefferson Hall to share successes, disappointments, and pranks.

____   ____   10. **Backboard Fever:** It's nonstop basket-ball excitement! Chip and Mary Hilton face a personal crisis. The Bollingers discover what it means to be a family, but not until tragedy strikes their two sons.

____   ____   11. **Fence Busters:** Can the famous freshman baseball team live up to the sportswriter's nickname or will it fold? Will big egos and an injury to Chip Hilton divide the team? Can a beanball straighten out an errant player?

____   ____   12. **Ten Seconds to Play!** When Chip Hilton accepts a job as a counselor at Camp All-America, the last thing he expects to run into is a football problem. The appearance of a junior receiver at State University causes Coach Curly Ralston a surprise football problem too.

I have   I expect
read: to read:

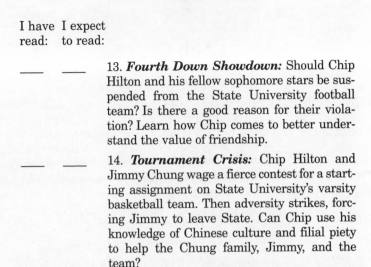

_____ _____ 13. ***Fourth Down Showdown:*** Should Chip
Hilton and his fellow sophomore stars be sus-
pended from the State University football
team? Is there a good reason for their violation? Learn how Chip comes to better understand the value of friendship.

_____ _____ 14. ***Tournament Crisis:*** Chip Hilton and
Jimmy Chung wage a fierce contest for a starting assignment on State University's varsity
basketball team. Then adversity strikes, forcing Jimmy to leave State. Can Chip use his
knowledge of Chinese culture and filial piety
to help the Chung family, Jimmy, and the
team?

About the Author

CLAIR BEE, who coached football, baseball, and basketball at the collegiate level, is considered one of the greatest
basketball coaches of all time—both collegiate and professional. His winning percentage, 82.6, ranks first overall
among any major college coaches, past or present. His
name lives on forever in numerous halls of fame. The Coach
Clair Bee and Chip Hilton awards are presented annually
at the Basketball Hall of Fame honoring NCAA Division I
college coaches and players for their commitment to education, personal character, and service to others on and off
the court. Bee is the author of the twenty-three-volume,
best-selling Chip Hilton sports series, which has influenced
many sports and literary notables, including best-selling
author John Grisham.